THE HOUSE ON DAGGER POINT

THE BEACH HOUSE MYSTERY SERIES
BOOK 3

CHRISTY BARRITT

CHAPTER
ONE

UNRELENTING RAIN POUNDED Olivia Beaumont's car as her headlights illuminated the house in front of her.

She hadn't thought she was going to make it here. Not with the roads on the island flooding as they were. According to the guard manning the gated community, a boat had hit the pilings on the bridge over the Kiawah River.

The news had shocked her. Olivia had crossed that very bridge—the only way on and off the island—a mere fifteen minutes before the accident. The damaged structure would probably be shut down, which meant Olivia had gotten here just in time. The only problem was that now she'd be stuck here.

She'd known the weather would be bad, but she'd felt compelled to come. To get away. To hide.

Especially considering the last text she'd received.

You deserve to die. All your sins will be revealed. Just wait.

She frowned at the memory of those words.

Olivia certainly had her fair share of imperfections, but most were things invisible to the human eye. Bitterness. Unforgiveness. Self-righteousness.

But did she deserve to die?

The unknown sender's words had left her shaken to her core.

She stared ahead at the stilted three-story beach house where she'd be staying for the next week. The place was surrounded by mature magnolia and oak trees—at least, that's what she thought she'd seen through the driving rain and darkness.

The house itself had a vintage look about it, much older than most of the other homes here on Kiawah Island, South Carolina.

This was it. She frowned. This was the place where everything had gone down.

And the place that might offer answers, resolution, and closure.

Olivia let out a long breath. She'd deal with those thoughts in the morning. Right now, it was late, and she was tired after traveling all day from Raleigh.

She'd go inside, get some rest, and tackle her questions tomorrow.

With any luck, no one would know she'd come here. Olivia would be invisible during her time on the island. The fishbowl she'd been living in would become more of a closet where she could hide.

Still, a trickle of fear crept down her spine.

What if coming here was risky? What if she'd played into someone's scheme to get her here to this very place—someone who might want to hurt her?

She swallowed hard, hoping that wasn't the case. She prayed those text messages were just empty threats sent by a bitter—but harmless —enemy.

Olivia couldn't let those seeds of fear be planted in her mind.

That's what she always told her clients. *The mind is the biggest battlefield in any challenge. Don't plant something you don't want to grow.*

She stared out the windshield again as the rain pounded the glass.

The weather wasn't going to break anytime soon, so she'd have to either settle in to wait it out or run for it.

Decision made, she fished the house key from her purse.

After her father passed away, Olivia had found it in his desk, hidden in an envelope taped behind a drawer. A note tucked into the envelope listed an address and read: *Spare key hidden in outdoor shower. Can't wait to meet you there. XOXO*

She wasn't sure who he'd written the note to—only that it wasn't anyone in his family.

Gripping the key, Olivia opened her car door and darted through the chilly downpour to the front porch. The alcove did little to protect her from the driving rain.

She fumbled to insert the key into the lock, but finally it worked.

She shoved the door open and nearly tumbled into the darkness on the other side.

For a moment, her heart pounded erratically as black surrounded her.

Running a hand along the wall, she found the light switch and flipped the lights on.

Relief instantly filled her as a beautiful house came into view.

She shouldn't be surprised. Her father had always had excellent tastes.

Her stomach roiled at the memory of her father's "tastes."

He had destroyed so many lives. So many.
Including hers.

Olivia needed to find a bathroom and dry off. She was dripping wet. Though the place was stuffy, she still felt chilled.

Drawing in a hesitant breath, she stepped farther into the house.

Maybe it was the storm that had her spooked. Or the menacing texts.

Or maybe it was just the threats in general. Her life had been a strange mix of stress and walking on pincushions lately. She'd always lived under scrutiny, but even more so in recent weeks.

But being here . . . it already felt like the ghosts of her father's indiscretions haunted the space between these walls—and therefore her as well.

Moving deeper into the room, Olivia realized the first floor was more of a studio-style apartment with a kitchenette, a two-person table, a small couch, and a double bed tucked into the corner. There were few —if any—personal effects.

Lightning lit the room in a purple glow and thunder shook the walls. The storm outside easily reflected the storm tearing at her soul. Her emotions were so tumultuous, and she wasn't sure when the squall would pass.

Her gaze stopped at a staircase on the far side of the room.

Olivia felt hesitant as she ascended the steps, anxious to explore the next two levels. Wanting to see what the upstairs might hold. Fearing what it might be.

As she reached the door at the top of the stairs on the second floor, she twisted the handle.

It was locked.

She tried the key to no avail.

Frowning, she paused and considered her options.

She could simply stay downstairs tonight and figure out a way to get inside the rest of the house in the morning.

But Olivia was curious. She had too much adrenaline. She'd come too far to stop now.

Instead, she remembered the note she'd found in her father's desk. *Spare key is in the outdoor shower. Can't wait to meet you there. XOXO*

Though it was pouring rain outside, Olivia had nothing to lose at this point. She was already soaking wet.

Leaving her purse on the couch, she opened the door and darted outside again.

She knew many beach houses had outdoor showers so people could rinse off after a trip to the ocean. Usually, the stalls were located beneath or beside the house.

Using the light on her phone, Olivia shone the beam in front of her, on the lookout for any critters lurking nearby.

She'd done a small amount of research before

coming, and she'd read something about alligators being on the island.

Alligators? No thank you. Fortunately, her phone had a waterproof case because there was no way she was walking around outside in the dark while the Creature from the Black Lagoon could be right in front of her.

She hurried to the ground level and around the side of the house, rain pelting her with every step.

Passing a small storage shed, she spotted a wooden bin filled with boogie boards and sand buckets.

Then she spotted a stall door under the house.

A shower.

Olivia darted toward it, thankful to get out of the rain. After a few fumbling attempts, she managed to get the door unlatched.

She stepped inside and, as soon as the door swung shut behind her, the aroma of salt water and flowers surrounded her, along with . . . another scent.

Something almost putrid.

Had a sea creature crawled under here and died?

Her flashlight illuminated a switch on the wall. Olivia flipped it, and a dim light shone from above. Turning her phone off and sliding it into her pocket, she glanced around.

The space was divided into two sections—the first

featuring a small changing room with a bench and some hooks for towels.

Olivia ran her hand along the wooden beams framing the structure but didn't feel a key.

More thunder shook the sky. Olivia felt it all the way to her bones, and her soul seemed to rumble in harmony with it.

She needed to find this key and get back inside ASAP.

Adrenaline fueling her, she rushed into the shower area.

As she did, a scream caught in her throat.

A woman hung from the showerhead, her body limp and pale.

And dead.

Olivia stumbled backward, out of the shower stall.

As she did, a shadow moved beneath the house.

The shifting outline wasn't from the storm or swaying tree branches.

It was a man.

Olivia clutched her chest as her heart pounded out of control.

Had the killer returned to find another victim?

Anderson Scott wasn't sure what he was doing here.

He only knew he needed to do some soul-searching and that this island seemed like the perfect place to do so. That's what had led him to this house on this dismal, stormy evening.

Real estate agent and property manager Megan Robertson was supposed to meet him here—she'd told him ten minutes ago that she was on her way. When Anderson had pulled up to the house, he'd been surprised to see a car in the driveway and then the flashlight bobbing beneath the house.

Megan must have gotten here early and decided to either wait for him out of the rain or to check out something on the property.

As he ducked beneath the house toward the light, someone said, "Stay back."

He wiped the rain out of his eyes, unable to see who had spoken.

"Megan? It's just me." The roar of rain muted his voice. "I didn't mean to scare you. I saw your light down here and . . ."

"Did you do this to her?"

He blinked as a woman came into view. The thin blonde held something in her hands.

A gun?

The breath left his lungs.

No, that was a water hose.

Did you do this to her? Her words echoed in his mind.

At once, he forgot about how crazy the woman looked right now with her frantic eyes and water-hose gun.

Instead, alarms sounded in his mind. "What are you talking about?"

"Don't move." With her free hand, the woman raised her phone, and her fingers began punching the screen.

Her frightened eyes wavered back and forth from her phone to him. The next moment, she shoved the device to her ear, her hand shaking.

"Please, help. There's a woman dead in my shower, and I think the killer is standing in front of me."

A dead woman? A killer?

Was she talking about *him*? Did she think *Anderson* had killed someone?

With a lingering, cautious glance at her, he skirted past the woman to see for himself what was going on.

Anderson glanced at the shower stall behind her.

The breath left his lungs when he saw a woman dangling from the faucet.

He didn't need to check her pulse.

She was clearly dead.

No wonder the woman with the water hose looked so frightened.

He glanced back at her.

She lowered the phone, even though he could still hear the 911 operator on the other end. Suspicion lined her gaze as she lowered the water hose just slightly. But her body remained rigid as if ready to pounce if threatened.

"Everything is going to be okay." He patted the air with his hands. "I just pulled into town. I've never even been here before."

She continued to stare.

Anderson shifted, concerned for the woman. Based on her ashen skin and shallow breaths, she appeared to be going into shock. He'd seen it many times before.

"Do you know her?" He kept his voice firm but gentle, not wanting to upset her any further.

The woman's eyes suddenly glazed.

The hose clattered onto the concrete, and she started to sink to the ground.

Anderson grabbed her elbow to catch her. "You need to sit down."

He yanked a rainbow-colored beach chair from behind the shower and flicked it open. Then he lowered the woman into it and squatted in front of her.

His gaze locked with hers as he tried to keep her lucid. "I'm Anderson. What's your name?"

She still looked dazed, her chest rising and falling entirely too quickly for his comfort.

She didn't answer.

"Can you tell me your name?" Anderson repeated.

Finally, the woman's gaze met his. "Olivia."

So . . . she wasn't Megan. Good to know. Anderson had never seen Megan face-to-face, and he wasn't sure what she looked like.

"Olivia, I'm a firefighter," he continued, ignoring the thunder that rumbled overhead. "I have some experience with these types of situations. Do you know that woman in the shower?"

"No." Her hand covered the O of horror on her lips. "Who would do such a thing? Why? Why here?"

"I can't answer those questions." Anderson squeezed her hand. "But I won't let anyone hurt you. You're safe right now."

He had to stop her before panic set in.

But he had more questions—like what Olivia was doing beneath this house in the middle of a storm in the first place.

Before they could talk anymore, red and blue lights flashed against the bluish purple of the lightning.

The sheriff had arrived.

A small island had some advantages—like quick response times. His department back in Jacksonville, Florida, had prided themselves in making it on the scene within four to seven minutes.

They had it down to a science.

This, however, wasn't exactly how Anderson had expected the start of his trip to play out.

He'd come here to connect with his past—he hadn't planned on stumbling across a frantic woman and a dead body as well.

CHAPTER
TWO

OLIVIA THOUGHT she could trust the man kneeling in front of her—he'd seemed truly surprised to see the woman in the shower.

On the other hand, his timing was terrible.

As Olivia waited for the sheriff, the image of the dead woman remained in her mind—the *young* dead woman. She looked like she was only in her twenties. She had long dark hair, a slim build, and she wore a lavender bathing suit.

The pallor of death covered her pale, lifeless skin.

Lightning cracked the sky, sending another shiver down Olivia's spine. As the wind shifted, the putrid smell drifted her way.

The smell of death.

Nausea rose in her.

Thankfully, two deputies appeared at just that

moment. "I'm Deputy Beamer, and this is my colleague, Deputy Clinton. We got a call that you needed some help."

Still huddled in the beach chair, Olivia introduced herself as the homeowner and explained what she'd found.

Each new detail made more nausea churn in her gut.

The older of the two deputies, Beamer, a man with a square face and stout frame, paced into the shower stall. He stayed only a moment before walking back out. In the dim light, his face looked green.

"This area is officially a crime scene. Clinton, get some police tape." Beamer glanced back at Olivia. "You know the deceased?"

Olivia shook her head as she remembered the lifeless woman's face. "I've never seen her before. I just got here a few minutes ago. I've never even been to the island before, for that matter."

Clearly, Beamer didn't recognize the woman either. Did that mean she wasn't a local?

Could the dead woman be connected with her father?

More nausea churned inside Olivia until her dinner—a chicken Caesar wrap she'd grabbed in Charleston—began to come up. She inhaled several deep breaths, determined to remain in control and keep her dignity intact.

Anderson stepped closer to Beamer, his brow furrowed and his gaze distraught. "That woman . . . is she Megan Richardson, by chance?"

Olivia studied the man. He was handsome, with a square jaw, light brown hair that was cut short, and a fit build. She'd guess him to be in his early forties. His motions seemed steady and reasonable.

Had this Anderson guy come here to meet up with this woman? But, if that were the case, why wouldn't he recognize her dead body? Maybe the two of them had met online and had chosen this location to meet face-to-face for the first time. Had they planned on breaking in and using the house for a clandestine affair?

If that was true, Olivia wouldn't be surprised. As a family therapist, she'd dealt with situations like that more than she'd like to admit. The internet made it entirely too easy to cheat. Though she didn't see a wedding band on his finger, he could have taken it off.

Olivia tried to bite back the thoughts. She didn't even know if this guy was married or in a committed relationship. In fact, she knew nothing about the man. She hadn't always been so cynical, but life had changed her over the past several months, and now everything felt upside down.

"No, that's not Megan." Deputy Beamer narrowed his gaze as he faced Anderson. "How do you know Ms. Richardson?"

"I don't. Not really." He shrugged. "We've only talked online."

Only talked online? More red flags went up.

Beamer stared at Anderson another moment before nodding. "I'm going to need to see some ID from both of you. Then we need to search this area for evidence. Did either of you touch anything after you arrived?"

"We didn't arrive together," Olivia quickly said. "The two of us only just met. I walked around on the first floor a few minutes when I got here. I came out to the shower to look for a key to unlock the rest of the residence. I had reason to believe one was hidden in this area. That's when I found . . ." She rubbed her throat. "The woman."

"Anything look strange inside the house?"

She shrugged. "Not to me. But, like I said, I've never been here before."

Deputy Clinton emerged from the shower stall and stepped into their circle. "It looks like a suicide to me. Our victim is probably a tourist. Never seen her before."

"If you don't mind me asking, what indicates suicide?" Olivia waited, hoping the man would answer.

Her therapist brain churned. She'd dealt with suicidal people before. She hated to see things end like this.

Especially considering her father.

He'd overdosed and taken his own life.

Sometimes that realization still seemed surreal.

Maybe she should have helped him more. Maybe she shouldn't have been so harsh.

But this wasn't the time to think about that.

Clinton shrugged, looking surprised she'd thought to ask. "Hanging. That's a popular suicide method. She could have stood on the bench inside the shower to set up the situation, and then stepped off to . . ." He shrugged again. "You know."

That didn't seem like much of a theory to go on.

"Has anyone around here been reported missing?" Anderson joined the conversation also, his hands on his hips and concern in his gaze.

Beamer shook his head. "No, not within the past few months."

Thunder shook the air again, and Olivia scanned her surroundings, halfway expecting a killer to emerge from the shadows surrounding them. When no one did, she looked back at Beamer.

"Can you tell how long she's been dead?" Olivia asked. "Looks to me it's been at least a few days."

"Whoa!" Beamer let out a dry chuckle. "Armchair detectives? We won't have any information to give anyone until the coroner can examine the body and we run this woman's prints through the system. Until then, no more conjecture. We don't need rumors flying around the island."

Olivia let out a breath, not surprised by his response. "Understood."

But she desperately wanted more information. She *needed* it. Especially if she was going to stay here in this house on this island.

What if this mess was somehow connected to the other messes in her life? She wanted to think it was beyond the realm of possibility. But it wasn't.

Beamer frowned before turning back toward them. "Why don't you two wait inside? I'll have Clinton check out the ground floor first, just to make sure it's clear. But we're going to need to launch a full investigation into what happened. Backup is on the way, and it's going to take a while for us to document everything."

Beamer nodded to Clinton, who walked toward the front of the house.

Olivia glanced up at the man standing beside her—Anderson. He was supposed to wait inside with her. Did she even want him in her house? What was he doing here? That still wasn't clear.

Her impression so far was that he was meeting a woman named Megan in a rainstorm at ten at night at a house not belonging to him.

And who was Megan?

The questions made Olivia's head pound. She was overthinking this.

Maybe.

But this man had been kind. He'd helped her when she'd almost passed out. Had mentioned he was a firefighter—a noble profession.

Maybe Olivia was simply paranoid right now.

She shifted as a chilly breeze swept beneath the house.

Finally, she said, "I guess we should get out of the deputies' way so they can do their jobs."

"You're the homeowner, you said?" Anderson stared at her, a strange look on his face.

"That's right."

"I guess you didn't get Megan's message?"

"What message?" Olivia had no idea what he was talking about.

"Never mind." Anderson shrugged it off. "We'll figure out those details later. Getting inside sounds like a good idea. You should get some dry clothes on. You don't want to get sick."

Doubts immediately pummeled her, and her steps slowed as she questioned her decision to let this man inside her house.

What if Anderson was the person who'd sent her those threatening texts? What if he was simply a great actor who pretended to be innocent and clueless? After all, his timing was uncanny. He could have followed her.

Maybe she shouldn't have come here.

All Olivia wanted right now was to leave . . . but with the bridge out of commission and a storm raging around them, she couldn't.

No, she was trapped here with this stranger and a dead body during a raging storm in a house full of secrets.

After Deputy Clinton cleared the downstairs, Anderson stepped into the house with Olivia. He used his fingers to wipe the moisture from his face before scanning the place.

His breath caught.

The house was just as he'd envisioned it.

Thick load-bearing wood beams stretched across the ceiling. White wooden panels lined the walls. And the floor. . . it was a knotty wood, rough cut—

and it looked old, with gaps that had been filled with wood slivers and other patches.

As he studied the living room around him, Olivia moved across the room as if looking for something. A moment later, she grabbed some blankets from a basket near the couch. She handed one to him.

"You might want to put this around you," she said with a shiver. "Just so you don't get sick."

She took her own blanket—a turquoise one with seashells—and wrapped it over her shoulders.

He observed the woman more closely. Her blonde hair fell in waves below her shoulders, she had a thin, petite build, and her eyes appeared intelligent. He'd guess she was in her mid-thirties, and she had a soft Southern accent, reminding him slightly of Reese Witherspoon.

Did she really own this place? If so, what was she doing here now when he was supposed to be renting it?

She seemed to have the same thoughts about him. Except her thoughts may have gone deeper—to distrust.

Then again, she'd just seen a dead body. He couldn't blame her.

"I guess you didn't get the message . . ." he finally said, hoping to clear up why she seemed surprised to have him at her rental house.

Her gaze hardened as she glanced at him. "Wait . . . are you the one who sent me those texts? Did you follow me here?"

"Follow you? What texts?" At the sound of the accusation in her voice, another thought slammed into his mind.

What if Olivia had been sent here? What if she'd only made up that story about being the homeowner? He had learned the hard way that things weren't always as they seemed.

He narrowed his eyes, his guard instantly going up. "Wait . . . did someone put you up to this?"

She blinked in confusion. "Up to what? *You're* the one who showed up at *my* home."

They stared at each other a moment.

Something was seriously wrong here, and Anderson didn't like the uncertainty swirling in his gut.

"Anderson!" An emphatic voice cut into their standoff. "I'm so glad you got here before the bridge closed!"

His gaze swiveled toward the door.

A woman rushed inside, closing her blood-red umbrella before placing it in the corner. She shivered as she turned toward him.

"What's with the sheriff outside?" She stepped closer, and her gaze briefly wandered to Olivia before filling with confusion. "Oh, I'm so sorry. I thought you were coming . . . alone."

Anderson stiffened at the abrupt interruption. "Wait . . . Megan?"

The woman waved her hand in the air before laughing. "Oh, I'm so sorry. Where's my brain right now? Yes, I'm Megan. Pleasure to meet you."

Anderson shook her hand, unable to say it was a pleasure. Not all things considered.

Megan's gaze wandered to Olivia again. "And this is . . . ?"

Olivia crossed her arms over her chest. "Olivia— the owner of the house."

"What?" Megan's eyebrows shot up, and her cheeks flushed as guilt filled her gaze.

Anderson bristled at Olivia's words, not liking the facts that clicked in his mind. But he didn't want to jump to any conclusions either.

"I'm sure there's a logical explanation," he said. "Megan, you talked to her about me renting this place for the next month, right?"

"Renting it?" Olivia's voice climbed. "How is that possible? This place isn't a rental."

He turned to Megan, hoping she'd shed some light on this situation.

Instead, Megan frowned and rubbed her hands together, her earlier cheerfulness gone. "Oh, dear. I think we have a misunderstanding on our hands. Why don't we all sit down? It sounds like we need to talk before this escalates any further."

How had such a simple trip turned into this disaster?

Even worse—what if none of this was a coincidence? What if someone had set him up, and Anderson had walked right into their trap?

CHAPTER
THREE

OLIVIA STARED at the pair standing around her, ignoring the chill she felt. Ignoring the wet blouse clinging to her and the strands of hair stuck like glue to her face.

"Someone needs to explain what's going on here," she started, her voice firm just in case anyone tried to pull anything over on her.

The other woman—Megan—stepped forward with an outstretched arm. The woman was thirty-something and perky, with short, dark hair and a petite build.

"I'm so sorry," she started. "I'm Megan Richardson, and I'm a real estate agent as well as the property manager here."

"This property is being managed?" Olivia's thoughts raced.

She hadn't put all the details together yet. After all, she hadn't even known her father owned this house until she began to look through his list of assets two months ago. The media hadn't caught wind of this place yet—but it was just a matter of time before they descended like vultures.

"That's right. I've been looking after this property for the past six years. And you are?" Megan stared at her, a clueless expression on her face.

Olivia swallowed hard, not wanting to say her name. That reaction was such a change from the past when she'd been proud to be a part of her family. When her dad had been respected. When things had easily lined up for her because of her connections.

She found her voice and said, "I'm Olivia, Larry's daughter."

Megan's eyes widened as realization filled her gaze. "Oh . . . I see. Well . . . this is a little awkward."

"I still have no idea what's going on." Thunder crashed overhead as Olivia said the words, but she tried not to flinch.

What had she walked into? A dead body. A stranger renting the house. A realtor with her own agenda.

Then there were Anderson's words. *Who sent you here?*

What did that even mean? Was this man hiding some dark secrets? Was his timing a coincidence?

Bryson had always told her she too easily believed the best in people. For a long time, Olivia had considered that a good quality.

She no longer felt that way.

"I think I can clear all of this up." Megan clasped her hands together in front of her, looking like a lawyer about to make a closing argument. "Mr. Scott contacted me a couple of weeks ago and said he was looking for a place to stay here on the island. A discreet place."

"Discreet apparently defines this house." Olivia tried to keep the resentment out of her words, but she failed.

Megan let out another nervous laugh. "Anyway, no one has been here for a long time. So, I told Anderson he could rent the house. Of course, I had no idea you were coming. The property has been untouched for so long now . . ."

"You knew my father?" Olivia's heart raced as she stared at the woman.

Megan was pretty. Just the type Olivia's father may have chased after—despite the fact that he'd been married.

More nausea rose in her.

"Your father and I never met in person. He valued

privacy." Megan's face reddened slightly at the words, and she averted her gaze as if embarrassed.

Certainly, Megan knew about the scandal surrounding Olivia's father. If others had known Larry Beaumont was staying here, the connection had probably been the talk of the island.

"I feel like I've walked into the middle of a big misunderstanding." Anderson stepped back, an apologetic expression on his face. "Is there some-where else on the island I can stay, Megan?"

She frowned. "I'm sorry, but the island is fully booked this week. The popularity of Kiawah has been amazing for the tourism and economy of the island, but it's also a dead end for anyone looking for a last-minute deal."

He let out a long, burdened breath. "I'll go down to one of the other barrier islands in the area. I'm sure one of them has something open."

Megan held up her phone and frowned. "Ah, well . . . any other time I would say yes. But authorities just closed the bridge to the island. Unfortunately, you're going to be stuck here overnight at least."

"There's nowhere else he can stay?" Olivia clari-fied, unsure if she was understanding this correctly.

"I'm afraid not. This area is highly sought-after, and we book up months in advance." Megan's gaze wavered back and forth between the two of them before she let out another nervous laugh. "This is quite awkward now, isn't it?"

Olivia tried to get her thoughts under control. She'd come here to heal. To find answers. To be alone.

Not to share a house with a stranger.

Before they could brainstorm a solution, Deputy Beamer appeared in the doorway.

Olivia's shoulders tensed as she waited for his update.

None of this was what she'd envisioned when she'd decided to come here.

But it was just like she told her clients—sometimes you simply had to take what came your way and handle it with grace.

However, doing so seemed to be becoming harder and harder all the time. And with a dead body added to the mix . . . danger and uncertainty seemed to swirl in the air along with the tempest winds of the storm.

Anderson hated being in this position.

Coming to Kiawah Island had seemed like the perfect solution to his problems.

But now it was clear he'd been wrong.

He stared at Olivia as she studied him unapologetically.

Why did she seem familiar?

Anderson couldn't place it off the top of his head. He only knew he felt like he'd seen her somewhere before.

Deputy Beamer stepped closer, rain dripping from his parka and what seemed like a permanent frown on his face. He nodded at Megan. "Ms. Richardson."

"Hi, Orville."

He turned back to Olivia. "We're going to be out there a while. I also need to look around upstairs, just to make sure there's no evidence of a crime."

Megan's eyes widened. "A crime? I thought the sheriff was here because of the occupancy issue."

Beamer frowned again. "Unfortunately, it's more complicated than that. We have a dead body."

Megan gaped. "A dead body? Here on Kiawah Island? No . . ."

Olivia extended her arm behind her. "Feel free to look around. But I don't have a key to access the upstairs."

"I have one." Megan pulled it from her pocket and held it up as if she'd found the golden ticket at an Easter egg hunt.

As Beamer took it from her, Olivia turned to the

deputy. "Do you mind if I follow you upstairs? I promise to stay out of your way and not touch anything. It's just that I've never seen this place before and . . ."

"And what?" Beamer asked.

Her mouth opened then shut. "I don't know. I just need to see what's here."

Beamer considered her request a moment before nodding. "As long as you don't disturb anything, I suppose that should be fine. You'll need to stay behind me just in case there's evidence."

Anderson watched as she ascended the stairs behind Beamer.

He hoped she didn't make any other gruesome discoveries upstairs. She'd already been through enough surprises for one evening.

In fact, so had he.

He wasn't certain that the woman in the shower was suicidal either. And if that was the case . . . did that mean there was a killer on this island?

CHAPTER
FOUR

OLIVIA FOLLOWED DEPUTY BEAMER UPSTAIRS, dread pooling in her stomach.

She thought she'd feel relief at being allowed to follow the deputy. Instead, trepidation rose in her as she wondered what she might find.

Evidence of the crime? Of her father's affairs?

Or maybe even another threatening message?

As Beamer flipped on the lights upstairs, Olivia examined the home her father had kept hidden from his family.

Her throat tightened at the sight of the living room. At the faint smell of sandalwood, her father's favorite cologne. At the images of her dad being here while under the guise of a business trip.

This place had been part of his secret life. A life she'd had no idea existed.

Had her father brought women here?

Olivia recoiled with disgust at the thought.

Remaining behind Beamer, she paced deeper into the living room and paused near some bookshelves.

The pictures on the shelf . . . pictures of her family . . . her face, her brother's, and her mother's had been blackened—scribbled over—with a marker.

The air left her lungs.

Why . . . ?

Deputy Beamer appeared beside her and grunted as he followed her gaze. "Your family?"

"Yes." This was her family—back before they were broken.

But if her father was bringing other women here, why would he put out photos of his family? What sense did that make?

"Any idea who might do this?" Beamer asked.

"Too many people to name." Olivia shoved a hair behind her ear and glanced at the stairway. Anderson and Megan had followed them up.

She'd just wanted privacy, but that was apparently too much to ask. The last thing she wanted someone else to overhear was her shameful family secrets. Unfortunately, Megan seemed like the type who liked to talk and share juicy gossip.

"Any of those people have access to this place?" Beamer gave Olivia a hard stare.

"Not that I know of . . . but maybe."

Deputy Beamer glanced at Megan. "You said you've been managing this house, right? When was the last time you were here?"

"I try to come by every month or so to make sure everything is good. But it's probably been two months since I was here last. I was going to come first thing in the morning to make sure it was ready for Mr. Scott. Then he'd called and asked me to meet him tonight." Megan rubbed her throat. "Clearly, there was some miscommunication, however."

"When was the last time someone stayed here?" he continued.

She shifted, almost looking uncomfortable. "I'm . . . not sure. Maybe nine months ago."

"Do you remember who it was?"

"Mr. . . . Mr. Beaumont." She swiped a hair behind her ear.

Deputy Beamer's gaze darkened. "Seeing these pictures and evidence that someone has been inside, I'm going to need to check out the rest of this place. Alone. As in, you three stay where you are and don't touch anything."

Olivia wanted to see the rest of the house, but she could explore later. Instead, she nodded. "Of course."

She quickly thought about how the house had looked when she'd arrived.

There had been no obvious signs of forced entry. No signs of a crime being committed in here.

But what about the pictures that appeared to have been vandalized in a fit of rage?

What exactly was going on?

As lights from the sheriff's cruisers rotated outside and more thunder rumbled, Olivia realized that staying here could be dangerous to more than her emotions.

Olivia wanted to rewind and restart this evening.

If only that were possible.

"While the deputy checks out this place, I thought you might want to know that this house has a fascinating history." Megan clasped her hands in front of her, transforming back into a salesperson.

Thunder rolled overhead again, almost like a sound effect to a frightening story.

"Does it?" Olivia tried to appear interested, but it was hard when she had so many other things to consider. The dead body. The image of those blacked-out photos.

Someone had not only been inside this house, but they'd been vindictive.

And if someone had been in this house once, who

was to say this person couldn't get inside again? Maybe Olivia's father had given someone—or several someones—keys.

Either way, someone with definite anger issues had been here.

"Seacret Hideout was one of the first houses built here on the island," Megan started.

Seacret Hideout? Olivia didn't know that was the name of this place.

How appropriate.

"Back when it was built, the sand formed a spit out in the ocean, giving this area the name Dagger Point," Megan continued, seemingly oblivious to Olivia's disinterest. "A lot of shipwrecks occurred there."

"Suitable name then," Anderson said.

"Isn't it?" Megan nodded enthusiastically. "Even though the stretch of sand is gone, locals still call this area Dagger Point. Local lore has it that the original house was built out of wood from those very shipwrecks."

Olivia glanced around. If what Megan said was true, then this house *was* fascinating. She'd always loved places with rich histories. She and her father had been alike in that way.

She frowned, wishing she could erase every

quality of her dad that she'd inherited. She no longer wanted to be anything like him.

"However, about sixty years ago, there was a terrible fire, and this place burned down to its bones—killing a man and woman inside," Megan continued, her face animated. "The town didn't want the house to be demolished, so they kept these very bones in place and built it back up again. This place has been standing since then, updated several times."

Burnt down to the bones, huh?

Olivia could understand all too well what that was like.

Her entire life felt that way lately.

Coming here only served as a grim reminder that she couldn't escape the past no matter how far she ran.

But at least she was still alive, she still had the opportunity to fix things . . . unlike the woman in the shower.

CHAPTER
FIVE

EVEN AS ANDERSON'S curiosity grew, he knew Olivia's personal life was none of his business.

He tried to set his questions aside. But, still, he wanted to know who exactly this woman was, why she was so unfamiliar with this house she owned, and why she had so many unknown enemies—one of whom might have broken in to destroy her family photos.

A sense of danger lingered in the air—danger and mystery. Was the dead woman outside connected to any of this? Or had she truly committed suicide in a random stranger's shower?

Either way, it appeared he'd walked right into a real-life mystery. Too bad he'd been trying to escape any drama.

Deputy Beamer descended the stairs, his arrival a

welcome reprieve from Anderson's tumultuous thoughts.

"Things look okay up there," Beamer announced, speaking loudly to be heard over the rain pounding on the tin roof and the wind as it howled against the house. "But we'll need to search the place for prints before we give you free rein."

Olivia tightened her arms across her chest. "Do whatever you have to."

Beamer leveled his gaze with her. "Just to clarify—no one you know has been here recently?"

"Like I said, I didn't know this place existed until two months ago. This is the first time I've seen the house. I have no idea what's happened here." Her voice sounded dull, maybe even disillusioned.

Beamer crossed his arms as he paused in front of her, his ample belly protruding in the stance. "I assume you'll be staying here at least a few days?"

"I planned on it. Why?"

Beamer nodded. "We may have more questions."

"Whatever you need." Olivia let out a breath. "I am exhausted, however. Any idea how long it will be until I can take a shower and get some shut-eye?"

"Give us an hour to dust for prints, then you can have this place back. For now, wait downstairs."

Olivia, Anderson, and Megan headed back to the

apartment on the first level and stood facing each other.

Anderson tried to come up with a solution to their dilemma—*his* dilemma really.

Olivia had the rights to this place, not him. Even though he'd put down a hefty deposit to stay here, he'd talk to Megan about that later. There were other more important issues to address right now.

He pointed with his thumb to the front door. "You know what? I can spend the night in my truck tonight. It's not like I haven't slept in worse places. I was a Marine for ten years, after all."

"I hate for you to have to do that." Megan frowned before letting out a sigh and glancing around as if hopeful a solution would magically materialize. "Especially since this is my fault."

Olivia stared at them both, and, after a few seconds of thought, she crossed her arms again. "Megan . . . the two of us need to talk later. I don't like the idea that you planned to profit off my father's house without his permission. Or maybe you've been renting out the house all along?"

Megan's face heated again. "When we have more time, I'd be happy to explain."

The skeptical look remained in Olivia's eyes as she glanced back at Anderson. "And you . . . you can't stay in your truck tonight. Sleeping out there during this storm is a bad idea. And I understand this isn't your fault."

He glanced at Megan, unsure what to say. At least, she had the decency to look embarrassed.

"Since there are two separate living spaces, you can stay in the apartment here. It only makes sense."

Anderson offered a grim but grateful smile. "I'd hate to impose, but if you truly don't mind me staying tonight, I promise to be out of your hair as soon as the roads open."

"It's no problem." Olivia pushed a hair behind her ears, the dull look still lingering in her gaze. "As long as you know I'm not here to be social."

"That works fine because neither am I." In fact, that sounded perfect. *More* than perfect.

An unspoken agreement passed between them.

They'd have to work out more details in the morning.

For now, Anderson was grateful Olivia had mercy on him. Although he *could* sleep in his truck, he'd be much more comfortable in a bed.

But the secrets he felt lingering in the air would most likely mean he'd get very little sleep tonight.

Thirty minutes later, the sheriff informed Olivia they were finished upstairs, and Megan left—after giving Olivia her business card and the key to the upstairs.

During a break in the rain, Olivia and Anderson went to grab their overnight bags from their vehicles. As they did, Olivia noted all the first responder vehicles out front.

A fire truck had arrived, an ambulance, and two other sheriff's cars.

Anderson stopped and talked to several people, seeming to form an instant bond with the first responders. Maybe he wasn't a bad guy.

But, still, she had to be cautious.

Olivia had a feeling everyone would be outside investigating for longer, maybe even several more hours.

Bag in hand, she came back inside, Anderson following behind her. The pleasant scent of his sage cologne mixed with the salty smell of rain and the ocean.

She paused at the bottom of the stairs and turned toward him. His hair was damp with droplets between the strands.

Awkwardness jostled between them.

Olivia shouldn't feel awkward. She simply needed to view this as a rental house where two different people rented two different spaces. A locked door would separate them, and nothing about Anderson raised any red flags.

Except for the fact that he'd asked, "Who sent you here?"

It almost sounded like someone was after him.

She cleared her throat as she glanced at this stranger she'd been thrown together with. "It's been quite the night."

"That's an understatement." He let out a dry, almost sarcastic chuckle.

"Hopefully, everything will be cleared up in the morning, and the sheriff will have more answers for us. In the meantime, we'll make the best of things. Right?"

"Yes, let's hope. Thank you again for letting me stay here. I honestly thought that this place was a rental. I had no idea it was a private residence."

"I understand." At least the man was polite, Olivia mused.

"Good night, then." He nodded toward her, a tight smile across his face.

"Good night." Olivia grabbed her bag and purse and headed upstairs. Part of her dreaded being up there alone. For so many reasons.

One of which was the dead woman downstairs.

She shivered.

Suicide?

Olivia supposed it was a possibility. According to the sheriff, no evidence of foul play had been discovered. But everything had left her unnerved. Why had the woman chosen Olivia's property to take her own life?

None of this made sense.

She locked the door behind her before wandering the perimeter of the space. Her gaze stopped on those blacked-out pictures.

Who would have come in here and done this?

Or what if her father had done this before he passed away?

Olivia sucked in a breath, the thought jarring her.

If that was the case, why? What kind of jagged emotions would he have been dealing with if he'd done something like that?

Her dad had spun an entirely different persona between his life in ministry and his life behind closed doors. He *had* to know what he'd been doing was wrong. If Olivia had to guess, he'd justified his actions until they felt normal. Even if that were true, he had to have moments when he'd realized the impact his behavior would eventually have on other people.

The tragedy of it all seemed especially ironic since her father had penned the best-seller *Be Your Authentic Self*. She'd even seen a copy of that book on the shelf near those pictures, along with *The God of Mercy, Casting Stones,* and *Building a Strong Marriage.*

Olivia let out a sigh and closed her eyes, trying to keep her frazzled emotions in check.

Had one of the women her father scammed come back and destroyed those photos?

Or worse—had one of them killed that woman in the shower in an act of rage?

Olivia's lungs tightened until she could hardly breathe.

She'd been receiving hate mail since her father's scandal had been exposed. Larry Beaumont had at least six victims. If Olivia had to guess, more were out there—more who were just waiting to come forward.

This firestorm was far from being over.

She picked up one of the pictures from the shelf and stared at it.

The blacked-out photo of her family was taken on a trip to Cabo San Lucas, where they all stood on the beach smiling and looking like the perfect family.

If Olivia remembered correctly, this photo had been used in a magazine article about her dad—before he'd fallen. Back in his heyday. Back when people used to think he was right next to God in terms of perfection.

People had put him up on a pedestal, and he'd eaten it up.

On occasion, Olivia had heard her mom say that her dad wasn't the same person she'd married nearly forty years ago. Somehow, the popularity he'd gained had gone to his head and made him feel untouchable. He'd probably always had a touch of narcissism. But the power trip he'd gotten as a result of his success had only added to that.

Olivia set the frame back on the shelf with a thud.

She should try to get some rest.

While she was here, she figured she'd pack any personal belongings before putting the house on the market. Then she'd use those funds from the sale to repay the money her father had taken from people. She, her mother, and her brother had already discussed it.

A lot of money was unaccounted for. From what she'd gathered, her father had taken all the money supposedly going to a nonprofit to help the poor in Africa and kept it for himself. But where had it all gone? Could he possibly have owned other houses she didn't know about yet?

The thought didn't sit well with her. What else didn't she know about her father?

And, of course, Olivia couldn't deny that she'd come here, in part, to escape. After the scandal broke, people had camped outside her home. She'd had to change her phone number. An online petition had even been started to shut down her nonprofit.

As her phone buzzed, she glanced at the screen. She fully expected to see a text from her mom or maybe Cynthia Bertram, the one true friend Olivia still had after everything had gone down.

Instead, an unknown number filled her screen.

She braced herself for whatever the message might read.

Lately, texts from unknown numbers weren't good. Even though Olivia changed her number, the messages still kept coming.

This one didn't prove to be an exception.

God's vengeance isn't enough. He's asked me to help enact justice. Get ready. Or better yet—don't.

CHAPTER
SIX

OLIVIA COULDN'T SLEEP.

Couldn't stop thinking about what might have happened in this house.

About the dead body.

About the pictures.

About the threats.

About how her father had lost his soul here in this house.

Finally, at 3:30 a.m., she rose and pulled on a sweatshirt. Suddenly, the house seemed suffocating, and every shadow felt like a ghost.

The storm had passed, so she opened the sliding door and slipped outside on the deck. A cool breeze greeted her along with the sound of crashing waves in the distance.

There were no outdoor lights here—their beams

were bad for the sea turtles coming ashore at night to nest. Blackness surrounded her instead.

For a moment, Olivia felt unnerved and exposed.

Especially when she remembered the dead body again.

She couldn't stop thinking about that woman.

Who was she? What had happened to her?

It didn't matter if her death was suicide or murder, the loss of her life was still tragic. A family somewhere would soon get devastating news, and their lives would never be the same.

That wasn't okay. People's pain was never okay.

Olivia frowned.

Maybe coming here had been a mistake.

So many things felt that way lately.

But she could never have anticipated finding a dead body on this property. Somehow, Olivia had been unofficially designated to clean up this mess. By her mother because she'd been shattered and broken. By her brother because he'd distanced himself.

Olivia let out a sigh and closed her eyes.

When she opened them again, faint lightning lit the sky in the distance. The storm was offshore, but its light still spread across the ocean and illuminated the waves with their rolling whitecaps.

The beach had always been her place of peace.

Her dad wouldn't ruin that for her. She wouldn't let him.

She had some things to figure out while she was here.

Not only with coming to terms with what her father had done. Olivia needed to figure out her future as well.

She'd dedicated her entire adult life to caring for families in ministry. She'd worked with them, helping them through the pressure, the disillusionment, the fear.

Some studies showed that 70 percent of pastors felt lonely and like they had no close friends. Those feelings often bled into their families as well, creating hidden mental health issues.

That's why Olivia had begun blogging about topics relating to the subject. Eventually, after five years of growing her blog, she'd started a radio program. Then she'd gotten a book contract—three of them, to be exact. She'd broadened her area of expertise to include a wider audience, telling people in church how to minister to the minister.

Now, she felt like a hypocrite. Not just because other people had called her integrity into question.

All along, she'd told people that the rewards of ministry were worth the heartache.

Now she wasn't so sure. Now she just wanted to

tell everyone to jump ship. To forget about their callings.

Her feelings weren't healthy.

She swallowed hard, fighting back tears. The firm foundation under her was now shattered.

As another burst of electricity filled the sky, Olivia stilled.

Two people stood on the beach in front of her house. She was certain she'd seen them until darkness had drawn the curtain again and they disappeared.

Her lungs froze, and she edged back against the house as she waited for another glimpse.

She needed to confirm what she'd seen.

Who would be on the beach at this hour? Maybe a neighbor. Other houses did line this street, after all. There was nothing illegal about taking a late-night walk.

But considering the dead body downstairs, Olivia needed to be cautious.

Finally, lightning flashed in the air again.

The two figures appeared. One broad. The other petite.

They faced each other as if talking.

Olivia squinted.

Wait . . . was that Anderson?

She couldn't be sure. But he was broad enough to fit this description.

And the woman . . . could she be Megan? Her outline was petite, just like the realtor.

Why in the world would the two of them be meeting at this hour?

Tension climbed up Olivia's spine.

The next burst of lightning showed the man had turned and started back toward the house. Maybe it *was* Anderson.

Quickly, Olivia slipped back inside, locked the door, and pulled the curtains.

What was going on?

And who exactly had she invited into her home?

The next morning, Anderson was thankful to find some coffee waiting to be brewed beside the pot in his small kitchenette. He prepared some, willing to drink it black.

He'd been a firefighter for twelve years, so he was used to drinking strong coffee. Only in the past two years had he taken to adding anything into the liquid —heavy cream and cinnamon, preferably. Once he'd neared forty, his friends had told him to be proactive, to go low carb and high fat. He hated it and had only half committed. Thankfully, he wasn't battling the bulge yet.

But beggars couldn't be choosers, as the saying went, and he didn't feel like running to the store right now for any cream.

He had too much on his mind.

Even before the events of last night, he'd had too much to think about. His life was in turmoil, and the only source of comfort he'd found was in the idea of getting back to his roots. That desire had led him here.

Clearly, coming hadn't been a good idea.

Last night's storm had passed, and, as he waited for the coffee to finish brewing, he gazed through the window and saw the gray sky and swaying trees. A large dune blocked the view of the ocean.

He decided to step out onto the deck to clear his head and form a game plan.

He'd need to locate an alternate place to stay for the remainder of his time here. If Megan couldn't find anywhere for him, he'd have no choice but to leave once the bridge opened again.

Yet, he'd planned on being away for at least a month. He simply needed time by himself.

No, not just to himself.

He needed time at this property.

A property that went back several generations in his family.

He pushed the sliding glass door open and stepped out.

But when Anderson glanced at the wooden boards beneath him, he stopped in his tracks.

Footprints stained the deck.

He squatted for a better look.

Those weren't just wet footprints. They had color to them—brown tinged with red.

Those were *bloody* footprints, he realized.

His heart pounded harder.

Just what was going on at this house?

CHAPTER
SEVEN

"GOOD MORNING," someone called from above.

Anderson's heart kicked up a notch as he glanced at the deck stretching over him.

Olivia.

She looked down at him, her hair blowing with the breeze and almost looking like a lion's mane. She didn't sound overly friendly—more matter of fact.

"I didn't want to scare you," she explained. "So, I thought I'd let you know I was up here."

Anderson hated to be the bearer of bad news, but he couldn't keep this from her . . . "We have another problem."

She disappeared before reappearing at the base of the outdoor stairway. Anderson quickly strode across the deck to meet her.

"What's going on?" A knot of suspicion formed between her eyes.

He nodded behind him. "Stay back. You don't want to disturb any evidence."

"Evidence?" She gasped as she glanced at the footprints near his door. "What? That looks like . . ."

"Blood," he finished. He pulled his phone out to call the cops.

Olivia ran a hand over her face as horror rolled over her features. "I just don't understand."

"You're not the only one." The dispatcher picked up, and Anderson explained what was happening. The woman on the other end promised to send someone.

"Where did the footprints come from?" Olivia followed the steps with her gaze.

"From what I can gather, they came from below the house and stopped at the sliding door. It was locked this morning with the safety bar in place, so no one got inside."

"Is there . . . ?" She shivered as she glanced at the dune. "Something dead down there?"

He knew what she really meant: is there *someone* dead down there.

"Maybe it's best if we let the sheriff look." He nodded toward the stairs leading to the second-level deck. "Why don't we wait upstairs?"

The suggestion wasn't only about preserving the evidence. He also wanted to get Olivia away from the sight of this.

She'd already seen a lot—been through a lot.

Anderson was no stranger to scenes like this.

As a firefighter, he'd seen terrible things. But there was no need to taint Olivia's mind and thoughts as well.

In other circumstances, he'd go check things out. But right now, he wanted to keep Olivia calm. So, he followed as she climbed back up the stairs.

She went to the railing, briefly glancing at the ocean before looking at the ground below—no doubt searching for evidence of a crime.

That dazed look returned to her gaze, just like last night when she'd nearly gone into shock. He needed to distract her.

"The sheriff should be here soon." He stood close, ready to catch her if she fell. "In the meantime, how did you sleep last night?"

She frowned. "Not great. You?"

"Not great either. Too much on my mind."

Anderson rested his elbows on the wooden railing as he peered at the ocean in the distance—an ocean that looked angry.

But even if the water was angry, it was beautiful. A sight to behold.

He observed Olivia another moment. This morning, she wore casual cream-colored pants and a black tank top. Her hair blew in the breeze, and her skin had a sun-kissed look to it.

She looked beautiful . . . and somehow familiar.

Anderson had been tempted to look her up online last night to satisfy his curiosity. But he hadn't. It seemed as if Olivia had come here to get some privacy also, and he didn't want to be the one to disturb that.

"I already feel calmer just seeing the ocean and smelling the salt air." He kept his face toward the salty breeze coming off the water.

"Me too. To be honest, I didn't think I'd like it here. But right now, in this moment—if I could just forget all my other problems, I might actually feel like I could breathe."

He was curious about what that meant.

What other problems had Olivia fled from? She'd also mentioned enemies last night.

Was she a famous actress? Singer? A secret princess? Reality show star?

That answer was none of his business.

If Anderson was smart, he'd keep that in the back of his mind.

The last thing he needed was to add more trouble to an already unwanted list.

But considering those bloody footprints . . . it was already too late.

Olivia couldn't get the image of the footprints out of her mind. Had a grisly act occurred last night? Was there another dead body out there somewhere?

Her skin crawled at the thought, but all she could do was wait for the police to check things out.

Until then, she tried to focus on something more calming—the ocean.

She knew from her years as a therapist that sometimes the ocean was just the medicine a person needed to help heal their souls.

The ocean and Jesus.

But now that seemed uncertain.

Olivia hated that she was letting her circumstances dictate her beliefs. At her core, she knew that wasn't the way things should work. However, when she was honest with herself, she knew she shouldn't ignore her nagging doubts. She needed to face them head-on, to slay them. Not ignore them.

She'd been determined to be more positive today. But now she'd seen those footprints . . . the bloody footprints.

What was going on here?

Maybe Olivia should run as soon as she had a chance.

But, for now, she needed to remain on the balcony with Anderson and wait for the sheriff.

She knew Anderson was trying to distract her by having casual conversation. It wasn't actually a bad idea.

She glanced at Anderson, curious about the man with his serious—almost haunted—eyes. But she refused to ask any questions. Refused to pry. To get involved.

She fixed other people for a living. But she wasn't here to fix Anderson.

She'd come here with the intention of fixing herself. That was going to require all her energy—and maybe even a little more.

"Megan is supposed to stop by this morning." Olivia drew in a deep breath. "I texted her last night before I went to bed to ask her if there were any security cameras around the place. She said there's one camera by the downstairs door, and she'll download any times it was activated in the past three months. Any further back than that, the videos are erased. Anyway, she said the file was too large to email so she would bring it by."

Anderson raised his eyebrows. "Smart thinking.

I'm sure the sheriff's department has probably asked for that also."

"She said they had. But I need to know what's going on here too. Maybe I'm a little too proactive for my own good, but I've never been someone who lets life dictate my actions. I like to call the shots."

She saw the questions in Anderson's gaze, but he didn't ask them.

Still, she knew they had a lot to talk about. Why he was here. What he was going to do. Who he was—who he *really* was.

She hadn't heard whether or not the bridge was open yet. But considering the fact a boat had hit the pilings, the chances seemed unlikely.

Did that mean the only way off this island right now was by boat? And if she left by boat, she'd have to leave her car here, which presented a whole other set of problems.

Olivia's thoughts continued to churn.

As she glanced at the beach, she paused.

Something tossed in the waves at the shoreline.

She'd heard about dolphins or other sea creatures washing up on occasion.

Was that what she was seeing?

Anderson followed her gaze. "What *is* that?"

"That's what I am trying to figure out also. It's pretty big, whatever it is."

Anderson's breath caught beside her.

"What?" Did he see something that she didn't?

He started toward the stairs. "Call 911. We need more than the sheriff—we need an ambulance out here."

"What's going on?"

"I'm nearly certain that's a person."

CHAPTER
EIGHT

ANDERSON TORE across the dune toward the ocean. The water wasn't far away, but it felt nearly unreachable.

His feet dug into the sand as soon as he stepped off of the wooden beach walkover. The deep sand slowed him down considerably. Pushing himself harder, he darted toward the ocean.

As soon as he reached the water, he dove in.

The body he'd seen being tossed by the waves had been drawn back into the powerful ocean.

As he surfaced, he spotted the woman. In a few quick strokes, he reached her and wrapped an arm around her chest. He swam with her back to the shore before laying her limp body on the sand.

When he saw the woman's expressionless face, the breath left his lungs.

Megan.

No . . .

He pressed his finger on her neck, hoping to find a pulse.

There was nothing.

He began chest compressions.

In the distance, sirens wailed as they headed this way.

Then Olivia appeared, dropping into the sand beside him.

She let out a gasp as she glanced at Megan and recognition washed over her. "What happened?"

"I don't know." Anderson sucked in a breath as water dripped from him and sand clung to any exposed skin. "I'm going to keep doing CPR until paramedics get here. But it doesn't look good."

Olivia clutched her heart before closing her eyes as if praying. "I can't believe this."

Neither could Anderson.

Hands still doing chest compressions, he quickly observed the woman.

She was fully dressed in a pale pink skirt and matching blouse. It was almost as if she'd been on her way somewhere when a wave had pulled her under. But why would she wear an outfit like this on the beach?

She wouldn't.

Nor was this what she'd worn yesterday.

Had something happened this morning?

His gaze went to a nasty bump on her forehead.

Anderson's heart beat harder.

Had someone done this to her?

At once, the peaceful day he'd envisioned faded completely from his thoughts.

Olivia stood near the dune and watched as paramedics took Megan's sheet-draped body away on a stretcher.

Anderson stood beside her, looking just as distraught as she felt.

None of this seemed possible.

The dead woman under her house.

The blacked-out pictures.

The bloody footprints.

And now Megan?

God's vengeance isn't enough. He's asked me to help enact justice. Get ready. Or better yet—don't.

Olivia shivered as she remembered the text.

Deputy Beamer approached them, sweat already beading across his forehead as he paused in front of them. "I don't know what's going on here, but I don't like it."

"Neither do I," Olivia assured him.

"None of it occurred until you came." He narrowed his eyes in scrutiny.

"That's not really fair." Anderson stepped forward with his hands on his hips, forming a formidable picture. "Olivia had nothing to do with any of this."

Beamer turned his gaze on Anderson, suspicion lingering in his gaze. "How do you know?"

"Because I've been with her. I've seen the shock on her face. I saw her almost pass out."

Beamer grunted as if he didn't buy that explanation.

Olivia cleared her throat, needing to change the direction of this conversation. "Did she drown?"

"We don't know yet." Beamer's gaze remained icy. "But if I had to guess she's been in the ocean for several hours already."

Olivia tried not to bristle at his undertones. "What about the woman in the shower last night? Have you IDed her yet?"

Beamer shook his head, taking out some sunglasses tucked into his shirt pocket and pushing them over his eyes. "Not yet. We haven't been able to get the coroner here. Hopefully, the bridge will open soon."

"Hopefully." Olivia rubbed her arms as another

chill washed over her.

"What about those footprints on the deck?" Beamer continued. "Any idea who they belong to? Ms. Richardson didn't have any wounds on her per se."

Olivia rubbed her neck, feeling a tension headache coming on. "No, but maybe the killer left the prints. Megan was supposed to bring me the security camera footage from the front of the house. There's a webcam on the doorbell that's motion-activated. Did she get you that footage?"

Beamer scowled. "No. She said the camera's battery went dead several days ago and that it's offline now. In the meantime, we're testing the substance comprising those footprints. We'll also see if the footprint matches any we have on file."

That seemed like searching for a needle in a haystack as the saying went. But Olivia didn't say that.

Beamer studied both of them. "Did either of you hear anything out here last night?"

"I didn't," Anderson said.

"I . . . I didn't hear anything," Olivia said. "But I *did* see two people out on the beach around 3:30. I couldn't ID them, however."

She wanted to blurt that one of them could have been Anderson. But she kept the words silent.

The man *had* just defended her, and she didn't feel right throwing him under the bus.

Not yet at least.

Beamer nodded slowly, almost as if trying to be intimidating.

It didn't work.

"Can you describe either of these people?" he asked.

"One appeared to be a woman. She was petite. I think she had short hair, but it was hard to tell."

"So, it could have been Megan?"

Olivia nodded. "Yes, it could have been."

"And the other person?"

"He appeared to be a man. Tall. Broad. Athletic based on the way he easily moved through the sand." *Someone who looked like Anderson.*

She didn't say that, though.

"Could you see what they were doing?" Beamer asked.

"Talking. Maybe arguing. Then the man stormed away from the beach."

"And headed where?"

Olivia swallowed hard. "He came in this direction. I didn't see anything after that."

Beamer cast her another skeptical glance before nodding. "I'd tell you both that you need to stick around. But I guess you can't go anywhere."

Olivia bit back a frown. "I guess we can't."

"I'm sure I'll have more questions. For now, I'm going to go check out those footprints again."

After Beamer walked away, Anderson turned toward Olivia and studied her face. "Are you sure you're okay?"

The concern in his voice touched her. Olivia was used to being the one taking care of others. She was the one people came to when they were at their lowest.

Somehow, people never really thought to ask her how she was doing.

She realized Anderson was still waiting for her response. "This is all just so crazy. I . . . I don't know how I'm doing, to be honest."

He rubbed his jaw. "I just can't believe this happened to Megan."

The late-night rendezvous Olivia had seen on the beach filled her thoughts.

She thought she'd seen Anderson heading back toward the house, leaving the woman he'd been standing with safely on the beach.

But what if he'd gone back?

What if Anderson had done something to Megan?

Olivia frowned as the wind pushed her hair from her face. Megan had lied when she'd said no one had been here for the past nine months, hadn't she?

Something was going on here at this house, and she wanted to know what.

"I have a feeling Megan was using this place for her own gain since my father, who owned this place, passed away." Her voice tightened with tension. "No telling how many people she rented the place to over the past few months."

"I didn't know about your father." Anderson softened his voice. "I'm sorry for your loss."

Olivia nodded, not sure what to say. She missed her father. But she wished things hadn't ended with so many hard feelings and unanswered questions.

Her dad hadn't been the person she'd thought. He'd fallen from grace and hadn't redeemed himself in the time before he died either. And nothing could change that.

"I'll get out of your hair as soon as I can," Anderson said.

Olivia pulled herself from her thoughts, realizing he'd taken her silence for irritation.

Did she want Anderson to get out of her hair as he'd said? She'd seen him meeting Megan on the beach. She'd seen the bloody footprints.

Yet, when Deputy Beamer had questioned him, Anderson hadn't mentioned meeting Megan last night.

Was this man trustworthy? Or was he more intricately entwined with the deadly events surrounding them than he was admitting?

Olivia stared at him and crossed her arms, deciding not to beat around the bush. Secrets . . . well, secrets had torn her life apart.

There was no reason to keep this one. She wouldn't tell Deputy Beamer about her suspicion, but she could talk to Anderson about it.

She squared her shoulders before saying, "I saw you last night."

He twisted his head. "When did you see me last night?"

"You were the man I saw on the beach at around 3:30. With the woman who looked like Megan."

A knot formed between his eyes. "I heard you telling the cops about that, but you're mistaken if you think it was me out there. I didn't meet with Megan last night."

"I didn't tell the cops it was you because I couldn't be sure. But it looked like you, and it looked like Megan. You started back this way after talking to her."

"Olivia . . . I didn't leave the house last night, and I definitely didn't meet with Megan." He shrugged. "I don't know what to say, but it wasn't me."

She raised her chin. "If not you, then who?"

"Maybe the person who left the bloody footprints? I don't know. I don't know what to tell you because I have no way to prove I'm telling the truth—only my word."

Olivia's back stiffened. "Maybe it would be better if you didn't stay here."

He stared at her a moment before nodding. "I'll do my best to find somewhere else to stay."

"That's a good idea."

Guilt pounded her. After seeing the way Anderson had so valiantly tried to save Megan, she wanted to believe he was righteous. But she had to be careful.

Believing the best in people had only worked to her detriment thus far in her life. She needed to learn from those past mistakes. Bryson had always harped on that point, almost wanting her to be more cynical. To be more guarded and less trusting.

She'd resisted at the time. But things seemed to be changing. She no longer knew who to trust.

A burst of wind swept across the ocean, sending a smattering of sand into her face.

Before she could turn away, she spotted Deputy Beamer heading her way again, and she braced herself for more questions.

More questions surrounding the fact that two dead bodies had turned up near her scandal-ridden residence in less than twenty-four hours.

CHAPTER
NINE

AFTER THE DEPUTY DISMISSED THEM, Olivia knew she needed to do something to distract herself—especially since running wasn't an option.

On a practical level, she knew she needed to unpack and get some groceries if she planned on staying here for the next week or so. Those tasks beat sitting around with her thoughts.

Deputy Clinton had told her there was a small market on the island. She would run there and get out of this house for a while.

After she showered and dressed, she headed outside. But as soon as Olivia stepped from her second-story entrance, she froze.

Was she seeing things or . . . ?

She hurried down the steps to her car and frowned.

Her tires . . . they'd been slashed.

The sinking feeling in her gut sunk even deeper.

Who would have done this? Had her car been like this earlier when the deputies were on scene? Surely, they would have said something to her if that were the case.

Then again, if someone had done this in broad daylight they were brazen—and that was something to be frightened about also.

At once, Olivia remembered that text she'd gotten last night.

God's vengeance isn't enough . . .

The hairs on her arms rose.

What if the sender watched her right now?

Olivia shivered as she glanced around.

She studied the tropical foliage surrounding the house. The curves of the landscape and the houses built on hilly sand dunes. The smooth driveway and the road beyond it.

She didn't see anyone suspicious.

She didn't see anyone at all for that matter.

But danger was clearly close.

Did the person who'd done this not want her to leave? Was that why he'd slashed her tires? Or was he simply trying to send a message?

Another shiver raced through her.

Then a new thought hit her. What if the next dead body was hers?

Just then, a footfall sounded behind her. Olivia nearly jumped out of her skin as she twirled toward the noise.

Anderson paused near the car, his hands raised in the air. Based on his shorts, T-shirt, running shoes, and AirPods, he was about to go running.

"I didn't mean to frighten you," he said. "I didn't know you were out here."

Olivia shook her head, her shoulders slumping. "I'm sorry. I'm just a little jumpy."

"Anyone in your shoes would be." He followed her gaze to her car. The next instant, he stepped closer almost in a protective gesture. "When did this happen?"

"I'm assuming it happened sometime after the deputies left. I came out here to take a trip to the grocery store and . . ."

He glanced back up, questions lingering in his blue-green gaze.

He had to wonder what was going on. What her story was. Even without the dead bodies, there were the blacked-out pictures and her cluelessness about this place, even though her family owned the house.

"Are you in danger?" he finally asked.

The question hung in the air and caused a knot to

form in her throat. It was the first time someone had asked her that point-blank.

Olivia wasn't sure how to answer.

"I don't know," she finally said.

Anderson stared at her car and frowned. "It looks like we need to call the sheriff again."

Olivia almost felt like a zombie as she nodded. So much had happened. She couldn't even wrap her mind around it all.

She wasn't sure if she'd ever be able to comprehend how her happy life had turned into such a disaster or how she'd come to have the sheriff on speed dial.

As Anderson watched Beamer and Clinton take pictures of Olivia's tires, he stood on the front steps with Olivia.

He didn't know what was going on, but Olivia was clearly spooked.

Though they were strangers, Anderson had a strong urge to help her—to protect her.

But there was clearly more to her story. Not only was the woman jumpy, but a preoccupied look stained her eyes.

Beamer approached Olivia. "Can I ask you a few questions?"

"Of course." But Olivia sounded stiff as she stood outside in the hot, muggy air. As the sun beat down on them, she slipped on her sunglasses. But was it because of the sun? Or was it because of the emotional turmoil inside her?

"I'll give you space." Anderson stepped onto the driveway, trying not to be nosy. But as part of Olivia's conversation drifted toward him, he couldn't help but listen.

"Is there anything else I need to know?" Beamer asked.

Olivia raised her phone and let out a heavy breath. "For the past month or so, I've been getting some threatening texts from various unknown numbers. But it's the same person. I can tell by the way the messages are worded."

Anderson's pulse quickened. What kind of texts had she been getting?

Deputy Beamer looked at her phone and grunted. "You have no idea who's sending these?"

She shook her head, her gaze hollow. "No, and the number is different every time. I think there's a computer program people can use to do that. It's like I said, I have a lot of enemies. Most of them, I couldn't even identify because they hide behind their computers."

"I'm going to need for you to get me a list of names of any you can. And I'd like for you to send me screenshots of these messages."

She pulled her arms tighter across her chest. "Of course. I'd be more than happy to do that. I can bring the names by the station later if that's okay."

"Sounds great."

A few minutes later, after Deputy Beamer pulled away, Olivia strode back toward Anderson. Her skin looked even paler than it had earlier, and her gaze was unsteady.

The hits just kept coming, didn't they?

"How about if I take you to get some groceries?" he offered.

Surprise flittered through her gaze. "I don't want to be any trouble."

"You're not. Besides, you let me stay at your place last night. I'm the one who's being trouble."

She didn't argue, but she didn't agree either. No doubt, she was questioning whether she could trust him. If she thought she'd seen him outside with Megan last night, then he couldn't blame her.

But that hadn't been him out there on the beach. He'd been telling the truth.

"I have a feeling it will take a while for new tires

to come in," he continued. "Considering the fact the bridge is still closed, who knows how long that will be? Besides, I need some groceries also."

Olivia stared at him another moment, uncertainty still in her gaze, before she finally nodded. "Okay. Thank you."

Anderson's jog would have to wait for another time. But he was okay with that.

Right now, he was more intrigued with this woman in front of him and what her story was. Even more, he was worried about her safety in light of everything that had happened.

Some type of internal voice whispered to him that her trouble wasn't over yet.

CHAPTER
TEN

OLIVIA NEEDED to distract herself from thoughts about dead bodies and bloody footprints—and threatening texts.

So, she studied Anderson's truck.

She'd always said she could tell a lot about a person by the way they kept their car.

Hers was neat and organized because she thrived on order and she hated chaos. Chaos—the very thing that seemed to define her life right now.

Anderson's truck was also neat and organized but clearly well used. Dry blades of grass dotted the rubber mat beneath her feet as well as some sand. An empty water bottle rested in the cupholder, and a pack of spearmint gum had been tucked away in the console.

The vehicle had leather seats, which she liked.

Several upgrades had been made to the interior, but not so many that Anderson seemed spoiled or indulgent.

As much as she wanted to like Anderson, she had to remember his timing was uncanny. He obviously had come here with some secrets as well. Until she knew what those were, she needed to keep her distance.

Why *had* he come here? Why had he requested privacy, as Megan had said? Why had he chosen her house?

She fought a frown at the thoughts.

The store was only about a five-minute drive away.

Olivia enjoyed looking at the houses around her as they traveled.

This really was a beautiful area—a planned luxury community that stretched ten miles. It was unlike other beaches she'd visited that were more sand-strewn and weathered. Here, lawns were perfectly manicured, the curbing was superb, and homes had an elegant vibe to them.

Kiawah Island was definitely an upscale community.

How had her dad even discovered this place? Her dad who had grown up poor. Who'd almost had to get food stamps during his first years in ministry.

Who believed people shouldn't go into debt or live extravagantly.

Olivia might not ever know the answer to that question.

"Do you golf?" Anderson's voice pulled her from her thoughts.

"Not really."

"Too bad. I hear there are some great courses here."

No, golfing had never interested her or her dad.

So, had he come here for the beaches? Or just for privacy?

Once at the store, she and Anderson paused near the front and turned toward each other.

"I just need to grab a few things, and then I can meet you back here." Olivia didn't want Anderson to feel obligated to walk with her.

"I want to grab some groceries also—some nonperishables that I can take with me when I find a new place. We can meet back here when we're both done. Sound good?"

"Sounds perfect." Olivia's lungs loosened as relief filled her.

Good. No awkward conversations. No forced proximity.

Although, could there be any more forced proximity than living with a stranger? Even if a locked door separated their spaces, the two of them had somehow been pushed together through no power of their own.

Olivia hoped the man would be able to find somewhere else to stay while he was here. She prayed Megan had been exaggerating when she'd said the island was booked to capacity.

As Olivia started toward the produce, she glanced at someone entering the store—a forty-something brunette whose eyes instantly went to Anderson. Approval lit her gaze.

Olivia wasn't surprised.

Anderson seemed to be that kind of guy. The type who could turn heads with his classic good looks and tall, muscular build. Of course, he'd get second glances.

She continued pushing her cart forward as her thoughts cascaded.

Bryson had been handsome but in a more buttoned-up way. On paper, their relationship had seemed perfect, like they were a match made in heaven, as the saying went.

But in reality, they'd almost felt more like friends than lovers. That wasn't always a bad thing. Marriage should start with a strong friendship. That's what she told people. But she'd always wanted more. She'd wanted passion and chemistry.

Though Bryson breaking up with her had hurt, it had also felt like a burden had been lifted. He was a sought-after motivational speaker, and suddenly being associated with her wasn't the best thing for his image or his career.

Olivia had known that someone who wouldn't stand beside her during these hard times was not someone she wanted to be linked with all her life.

As far as she was concerned, she and Bryson were done. Even though they were originally supposed to get married in the fall, she had to believe it was for the best that the wedding was off.

As her mind wandered, Olivia grabbed some bread. She had planned on being away only for a week, not that it really mattered if she stayed longer. Her career was on the rocks right now.

No one wanted advice from someone whose family was as messed up as Olivia's.

It wasn't that her family was entirely famous. Not to the masses, at least. But a strong pocket of people had followed her father on his radio program, through his books, and through his ministry at the church. They went to the conferences he'd put on and had been advocates for him online.

Until they'd been unable to deny the truth any longer.

When those people turned on her father, they'd

really turned. Not just on her father but on her whole family. Suddenly, they were all unredeemable villains, guilty by association.

Olivia grabbed some milk, put it in her cart, and tried to push away the bad memories.

There was one thing she'd known for sure when she had left Raleigh, and that was the fact she could no longer live there. She needed to start over somewhere. Start fresh.

It wasn't as if she had anyone to hold her down anymore.

Not since her mom had gone to visit some missionary friends in Africa for an extended period, her brother had distanced himself from the rest of the family, and Bryson had dumped Olivia.

She picked up a few more items, and as she wheeled her cart to the register, she felt eyes on her and stiffened.

She glanced over and saw the brunette from earlier staring at her.

Instantly, Olivia's cheeks heated.

Did the woman know who she was? Did she recognize Olivia?

She couldn't be sure.

Olivia tried to keep her chin up. But even as she did, she prayed there wouldn't be a nasty confrontation.

All she'd wanted was to disappear so she could heal in private.

That seemed an impossible wish.

Anderson had already paid for his groceries and waited near the front of the store for Olivia.

But, as she headed toward the line, she almost looked preoccupied, as if she didn't even see him.

She glanced across the grocery store, and Anderson followed her gaze.

A brunette stared at Olivia.

He recognized the woman because she'd accidentally run her cart into his and had giggled an apology. He'd seen the flirtatious look in her gaze, but he wasn't interested in dating or romance. Not after what had happened with Selena.

He stiffened as he continued to watch the interaction between the two women.

Was that recognition that flickered in the brunette's gaze?

As Olivia put her items on the counter, the woman muttered, "I can't believe you'd show your face here."

Olivia held her chin up higher and didn't respond. Instead, she almost pretended like she didn't hear as she turned to the cashier. "I need to get going."

The cashier, an older woman with short, gray hair, glanced up curiously and took her time scanning each item.

Anderson had the urge to step in, to help. But he didn't know what was going on. Didn't know how he could help.

A few minutes later, Olivia rushed toward him, three paper bags balanced at her hips and an anxious expression on her face. "There you are. I'm sorry if I took too long."

Her words sounded hurried, almost anxious.

"You're fine. Let me help." He took a couple of bags from her.

He helped Olivia load the groceries into the back of his truck before they climbed inside and started back toward the house.

Anderson wanted to ask Olivia on the brief ride back what that had been about, but he didn't.

They unloaded groceries at the house and he helped carry hers upstairs. Before Anderson went down to his apartment, he glanced out the massive windows overlooking the ocean.

Something in the distance caught his eye, and he paced toward the window.

"What is it?" Olivia crept closer to him.

But he didn't answer.

Instead, he focused on the dunes where a figure had just disappeared.

"Anderson?" Olivia's voice sounded strained.

He glanced at her, hesitation capturing him. He didn't want to give her this update. But he had no choice.

"Someone was standing on the dune," he finally said. "I think he was watching this place. But he ran. He was too far away for me to try to catch up with him."

Her face paled. "Maybe it was the person who killed Megan or the person who killed the woman I found in the shower. I don't care what the sheriff says —I don't believe that woman's death was suicide."

He didn't think it was either.

But he hadn't wanted to say those words in front of her.

The good news was that Olivia hadn't pointed the finger at him again. Maybe now that some time had passed, her suspicions about him had died down.

He could hope.

Olivia shivered as she stared out the window. From the heaviness in her gaze, Anderson knew she was wrestling with thoughts—with fears.

He gave her time to voice anything she needed to say aloud.

Finally, she said, "To be truthful, I don't feel entirely comfortable trusting the local sheriff's office to handle this. They seem inexperienced, like there isn't enough crime around here to give them the skill they need."

He agreed, but he hoped they were both underestimating the local law enforcement.

Whatever was going on here . . . it had him on edge, and he feared for Olivia's safety.

AS OLIVIA and Anderson stood on the deck, her thoughts raced through everything.

Could she really continue to stay at this house?

Did she have any other choice at this point?

Not really. Not until the bridge opened.

Before either of them could say anything, a woman appeared around the corner of the house. "Hi there!"

The bleached blonde had a cautious look on her face. She was probably in her thirties, and she wore jean shorts and a pink tank top that showed off her sun-kissed skin.

"I didn't mean to scare you, but I heard you up here talking." The woman stopped several feet away. "I'm Sheri. I live next door."

Olivia's muscles remained stiff. "Hi, Sheri. I'm Olivia. This is Anderson."

"Listen, I don't mean to impose, but I've seen a lot of law enforcement vehicles over here lately. Is everything okay?" She frowned as she waited for their answer.

Olivia glanced at Anderson and shrugged. "Not really."

Sheri's frown deepened. "Truthfully—I heard there was a dead woman found below your house. It's a small island. News travels fast. Then I heard about Megan. I just can't believe it." She shook her head, her cheerfulness disappearing.

"Neither can I." Olivia rubbed her arms, suddenly chilled despite the heat. "I'm surprised the sheriff didn't talk to you."

"I got a notice on my door for me to call them. But I haven't done so yet. It doesn't really matter. I haven't seen anything. Not really." She shifted, her arms pulled across her chest. "I'm surprised you can even stay here after all that. Kudos to you. I'd be entirely too creeped out by it all."

"With the bridge out, we don't really have much choice." Olivia shrugged again, not really in the mood to explain things to this stranger.

Sheri sighed. "I suppose you're right. This is all just so crazy. This island is usually so safe."

"How long have you lived here?" Olivia asked.

"Five years. My husband and I own the place next door, even though he stays in Charleston during the week for work and just comes here on weekends. It's a great little community . . . usually." She frowned again.

Anderson stepped closer. "Say, have you seen anyone around here acting suspicious recently?"

Olivia's heart rate skipped a beat as she waited for the woman to answer.

It was only smart to try to find out more information themselves. She mentally gave Anderson a pat on the back.

Sheri seemed to hesitate as if she were unsure whether or not to answer.

"We're just trying to understand what's going on," Olivia explained. "Have you seen anyone over at the house lately?"

Sheri leaned against the wall. "No, I used to see people coming and going every month or so. But that stopped about eight or nine months ago."

Olivia's face seemed to heat, and she rubbed her neck as if uncomfortable.

Was it because her theory about Megan was wrong?

She'd thought the woman was renting out this place, but maybe she hadn't been.

"I see," Olivia finally said. "But nothing since then?"

Sheri tapped her chin. "I mean, I did see Megan over here several times. But since she's a realtor in the area, her presence seemed normal."

Olivia straightened. "You saw her over here recently?"

Sheri shrugged. "She probably stopped by every week or so. Why?"

Olivia's thoughts raced.

She clearly remembered Megan saying she hadn't been to the house in the past two months.

So, someone was lying . . . and Olivia's bets were on Megan.

But the question of why remained.

Why would Megan lie about that?

***

"That was interesting," Anderson muttered when Sheri left a few minutes later.

Olivia crossed her arms. "It was, wasn't it? Why would Megan lie? I have to assume Sheri is telling the truth."

However, assumptions could be dangerous things . . .

Anderson frowned. "I have no idea. You think Megan had something going on at this place?"

Olivia stared at the ocean in the distance. "I don't know. But I suspect she was renting it out as a side gig. It's the only thing that makes sense, the only reason I can think of she would have said you could stay here even though this place wasn't officially on the market. I was hoping to talk to her some more, to find out some answers. That clearly won't be happening."

A frown pulled at Olivia's lips.

"So, it's all about making some extra money by having people stay here on the down low?" Anderson asked.

"I don't know. Of course, Sheri didn't say she saw other people here recently. She just said that she saw Megan. However, this house is hard to see from the neighbor's. There are too many trees. Besides, what else would Megan be doing here? If it was all above-board, then why didn't she just say so?"

"Those are all good questions."

"I want to go to the realty office." Olivia suddenly straightened. "I want to talk with some of Megan's coworkers and see if they know anything."

Anderson grabbed his keys from his pocket. "Since your car is out of commission, I'll drive you. I need to talk to them and see if there's anywhere else I can stay anyway."

Olivia stared at him, her frown deepening. "Look, you should just stay here tonight. There's a perfectly good apartment on the first level that's not being used with a locked door separating us. There's no need for you to find somewhere else. I was just reacting out of fear after Megan . . ."

He studied her face, looking for signs of sincerity. "As would anyone in your shoes. But I'm telling the truth when I said I wasn't meeting with Megan on the beach last night. I have no way of proving it but . . ."

She stared at the ocean as if reliving what she saw. "I can't even be sure that it was Megan out there. That's just how her profile struck me, but it was dark. Still, let's say it was Megan. What if the man she was meeting with was the killer? And the last time I saw him, he was walking this way. Then we found the bloody footprints . . ."

"I don't like the sound of that. Her death seems suspicious to me."

"I don't believe her death was an accident either. Not wearing those clothes. And if someone did kill her, then why? This has to be about more than her renting out this house without permission."

Anderson wanted to argue with her, but he couldn't. She was making some good points.

"I'll take you up on your offer to let me stay in the apartment. I appreciate it. Meanwhile, I say we go down to the realty office and see what they have to say," he finally said. "Maybe someone there will have some answers."

FIFTEEN MINUTES LATER, Olivia pointed to a white wooden building in the distance. "There it is. Sea Glass Realty."

Anderson pulled into the small parking area.

As Olivia stared at the office building, a rash of nerves fluttered through her.

She'd never pretended to be a detective. Had never wanted to be. In the past, if she'd ever hunted down clues it had been therapy-related, and the clues had been purely psychological.

But now life had dictated otherwise.

If something was going on in that house where she was staying, she needed to figure out what. That didn't mean she was going to launch a full-fledged investigation. She was just going to ask some questions.

This could all somehow tie in with her father's indiscretions. If that was the case, she needed to find those answers before the media did and published information about her family that would only further add to her mother's heartache. Her mother had already been through enough.

And if Olivia was honest with herself, so had she.

"Are you ready for this?" Anderson glanced over at her.

She snapped from her thoughts and nodded. "I guess I'm as ready as I'll ever be."

They climbed from his truck and walked to the front door. When they stepped inside, a young woman—probably fresh out of high school—glanced at them from behind the front desk. She lowered her cell phone, her gaze distracted.

Certainly, everyone here knew about Megan's death. This probably wasn't the most ideal timing to be asking questions, but they had little choice at this point.

Olivia approached the desk and softened her voice before saying, "I'm hoping to talk to one of the realtors here. Is anyone available?"

"Do you want to talk about renting a house? This is actually kind of a bad day. We had some sad news here at the office, and we're still trying to comprehend it. We lost someone who works here." Her lips flickered down as if she fought a frown.

"I'm so sorry to hear that," Olivia told her. "And it sounds like the timing truly is awful. However, this can't really wait."

The woman stared at Olivia a moment as if wondering about the meaning behind Olivia's words. Finally, she nodded. "Let me see who's available."

A moment later, a man stepped from the back office. He wore a white linen shirt that was unbuttoned halfway down his chest. He had shaggy blond hair with some gray mixed in.

Typical aging surfer. No doubt, he'd been handsome when he was younger. Truthfully, he was still handsome now in an older, more weathered way.

"My name is Duke Hastings." He plastered on a quick smile that didn't reach his eyes. "How can I help you?"

"I was hoping you might be willing to sit down with us for a moment," Olivia said. "It's about Megan."

His gaze instantly clouded . . . partly with caution and partly with grief.

Olivia wasn't sure if he would turn them away.

But she hoped that wasn't the case.

"Sure," he finally said. "But I have only a few minutes."

He led them into his office at the back of the building and closed the door. He then took a seat behind his desk while Anderson and Olivia sat across from him.

He leaned back in his chair, still studying them almost warily. "What can I do for you?"

Olivia swallowed hard as she prepared to launch into her questions.

Anderson sensed Olivia's nerves. But he admired the compassionate way she was handling this situation.

Part of him wanted to jump in and take the lead. But he didn't. This was Olivia's thing. It was her house, and he needed to proceed with that in mind.

"I'm the owner of 1892 Dagger Point," Olivia started, her neck muscles appearing slightly strained.

Duke's eyes widened with realization. "I see."

"I understand Megan was managing that property."

"That's right. That was one of the houses on her docket. But I'm not sure where you're going with this."

Olivia shifted and licked her lips before saying,

"I'm a little confused. To back up a little, my father owned this property, but until recently I didn't know it existed. However, my understanding was that the house was his private residence and not something rented out to others."

Duke's gaze remained steady as he seemed to consider her words. "I believe that's right. It's not on our rental list. I mean, I can double-check for you, but I'm nearly certain that's the case."

Olivia shifted. "So, here's where things get weird. Apparently, Megan was renting out the property."

Duke's twisted lips and tilted gaze made it clear he didn't believe her. "Megan wouldn't do that."

Anderson leaned forward, ready to back Olivia up. "Actually, she would. I called the office two weeks ago and inquired about renting that specific property. She told me I could. Then she met me at the house last night with the key so I could get inside. Unfortunately, other circumstances arose in the meantime."

Duke blinked several times as if confused. "That doesn't even sound like Megan. I don't know why she'd do that. Let me check something."

He turned toward his computer and typed several things in before shifting back toward them. "There are no records of that house being rented. We simply did maintenance on the property."

Anderson held up his phone. "She sent me a rental agreement."

Duke narrowed his eyes. "May I see?"

Anderson handed him the phone, and he let out a grunt. A moment later, he handed it back. "That is a rental agreement, but's it's not one of ours. This isn't in our files and, quite frankly, I'm stumped."

"Is it possible Megan was trying to make some extra money on the side since this is such a popular vacation spot?" Olivia said. "Could she have written up this contract herself—and been pocketing the money herself as well?

Duke seemed to think about the question a moment before shrugging. "I suppose it's possible. I don't want to speak ill of the dead. Megan has always been one of our best agents here. But I suppose we all have our secrets. Maybe she *was* trying to make some extra money and, if that's the case, I'm really sorry to hear that. That's not the way we operate around here."

At least he hadn't totally denied it.

"Do you think Megan kept any records to indicate who stayed at the house and when—unofficially?" Olivia asked. "Or maybe something to show who paid rent on the house during their stay?"

Duke sat up straighter. "If what you're telling me is true, I find it hard to believe she'd keep any records here at the office. She clearly didn't mention it to any of us here. She had to know she'd get fired if we found out."

"Are there any other reasons she might have been using the house?" Anderson's thoughts raced. He'd put down a hefty deposit on this place. He'd worry about getting that money back later—if he was able to get it at all.

Duke let out a long breath. "You're asking the wrong person. I really enjoyed having Megan as my coworker. But the two of us didn't chat about personal things very often."

"Does she have any good friends in the area she might have talked to about this?" Olivia leaned closer as if anticipating his answer, as if determined to find out something useful.

He seemed to think about it a moment before nodding. "Megan did hang out with Emma Jean. She works at Windswept, the restaurant at the Cypress Point Golf Club. If you want answers, you might want to talk to her."

Anderson stored that name away. He was certain that Olivia would want to talk to this Emma Jean.

"Now if there's nothing else . . ." Duke rose, suddenly looking exhausted. "We have a lot to sort through here at the office. I don't want to rake Megan's name through the mud, especially considering how fresh her death is. Any chance you guys could keep this quiet until you have more answers? Megan was a good woman. I don't want to see her legacy destroyed just because of an assumption."

Anderson could appreciate that. He could *really* appreciate it, for that matter.

"I'll be discreet," Olivia promised. "But in the meantime, if you find anything in her records about the house, would you mind letting me know?" She jotted down her name and number and handed over the paper.

Duke nodded curtly. "Will do. I hope you find some of those answers you're looking for."

OLIVIA WAS quiet as she and Anderson climbed back into his truck. She had a lot to think about—like how far she wanted to push this. Should she step back and let the cops take over? Or should she keep searching for answers herself?

Considering the threats on her life, it didn't seem like she had any choice but to keep trying to figure out what was going on herself. She was the one with the most at stake here.

"So, what now?" Anderson cranked the engine, allowing cooler air to blow through the vents, but he made no effort to leave. "You want to go to the golf club?"

Olivia frowned as she stared at the realty office another moment. "I do. But I promised Deputy

Beamer I'd make a list for him and drop it by his office."

"So . . . back to the house?"

Olivia glanced at him, uncertainty warring inside her. "I know I'm probably asking too much of you."

He shrugged in a laid-back manner. "Ask away. I didn't really have many plans when I came here."

She shifted toward him, her eyes wide and imploring. "How would you feel if I treated you to some coffee and made the list while we took a break? Then I could drop it off with Deputy Beamer before we head back?"

"Only under one condition."

She stared at him, something close to anxiety bubbling inside her. "What's that?"

"You've so graciously let me stay at your place. How about if I get us a reservation at Windswept tonight, and I treat you to dinner? That way you can eat, *and* you can talk to Emma Jean if she's working."

She turned over that idea in her mind, questioning how to respond. But she really had no reason to say no. "That sounds great, but you don't need to pay for my meal."

"It's really the least I can do."

Olivia stared at him a moment before finally nodding. Without any answers, she didn't know who she could trust, but something about Anderson made her want to trust him.

That wasn't something she'd often said over the past several months.

But it was clear she could use a friend while she was here on this island. She could use someone watching her back. Still, she'd need to be cautious around Anderson. But having dinner and getting to know him a little wouldn't hurt anything—not if Olivia was careful.

"Okay. That sounds nice."

"Perfect. For now, let's find a coffeehouse, and then I'll see if I can get that dinner reservation."

Olivia nodded, liking the sound of that plan. "Okay then. A vanilla latte is calling my name."

A grin stretched across Anderson's face. "Then we better go find you one."

Something about the way he said the words . . . about the faint smile on his face . . . it caused Olivia's pulse to quicken.

She didn't know why.

She wasn't interested in romance.

But if she were . . . someone like Anderson Scott would be at the top of her list.

Provided he wasn't the man she'd seen outside with Megan before the woman died.

Twenty minutes later, Anderson and Olivia were sitting at a quaint coffee shop among other patrons. The place was classy, with rich wooden floors, thick tables, and a high ceiling. The scent of cinnamon and java floated in the air, and a backdrop of whizzing frothers and murmuring patrons filled the air.

Anderson quickly surveyed everyone inside, but no one gave him and Olivia any particular attention—unlike what had happened at the grocery store.

Olivia had her vanilla latte, and he had his coffee with cream and cinnamon. He'd fished a notepad and pencil from the console of his truck, and Olivia now held that in front of her.

She took a sip of her drink as she stared at the blank page.

Anderson was anxious to see who might be on her list, but he didn't want to ask too many questions. He'd much rather Olivia volunteer that information.

She stared at the paper another moment before sighing and glancing up at him. "Before I start writing this list, I'm sure you're probably wondering what kind of list this even is."

"I think I recall you telling Deputy Beamer that it

was a list of your enemies. If you don't mind me asking, what makes you think you have enemies?"

Olivia nodded slowly, almost hesitantly. "We just found out nine months ago that my father had a string of affairs. He kept this place secret from us. Apparently, he brought women to the island for his little rendezvous."

His eyes widened before his lips tugged down in a frown. "I'm sorry to hear that."

"It was a shock to find out. I only came here to get the place ready to sell." She stared into her latte. "It definitely hasn't been an ideal situation, to say the least."

"You said he's passed away since then?"

She rubbed her throat, her entire body tensing. "He took his own life after his secrets were revealed. Apparently, he couldn't handle the consequences of his actions, so he left my mom, my brother, and I to handle it for him."

"I'm so sorry." Anderson gripped his coffee, wishing he could find something better to say. "I can't even imagine everything you're going through."

Olivia nodded, a dazed look in her gaze—dazed with grief and disappointment and pain. "Thank you. It's been a bit overwhelming, to say the least.

But when it comes to enemies, this is why I have many."

He shifted, sensing she wanted to talk. "How many women did your dad have affairs with?"

"At least six that I know about, though I suspect there are others who haven't come forward yet."

"Have some of these women made threats toward you?"

Her gaze clouded. "I've been getting some nasty texts. People are definitely holding my family accountable for my father's actions. They've said some really hateful things. So, I figured I'd start with these victims and their families"

"You said he had affairs. So, why are you calling the women victims?"

"My father was in a position of power over them. Though they were all of age and most of them probably knew he was married, he still used his position to manipulate them."

He nodded as understanding rolled over him. "I see."

"Anyway, they're the ones who have the most reason to want to hurt me."

Hurt me.

Her words echoed in Anderson's mind.

The things people would do for retribution . . . it never ceased to amaze him.

But hurting Olivia because of her father's actions? That wasn't okay.

OLIVIA HESITATED as she stared at the paper. Something about putting these names down in print made nausea roil inside her. The last thing she wanted was to villainize women who'd already been taken advantage of by her father.

But she had no other choice right now. She just needed to suck it up and get this done.

She wrote the first name. Starla Stevens.

The woman was fifty-six years old and a former fitness instructor. Olivia's father had counseled her in his office, and that's how their affair had begun. Starla was single and heartbroken over what had happened. But she didn't seem vengeful.

Nancy Waddell was the next victim. Nancy was in her forties and had been fresh out of a divorce when she'd met Olivia's father. Apparently, their affair had lasted five years.

The nausea grew stronger and stronger inside Olivia with every name.

Anderson's hand suddenly covered hers. "Are you sure you're going to be okay?"

She tried not to feel a jolt at his touch. But she'd be lying if she denied feeling something.

He seemed to notice her reaction—maybe even misread it—and he pulled his hand away. Instantly, Olivia missed his touch.

She swallowed hard and tried to stay focused. "This is just hard, to say the least."

He glanced at the list and raised his eyebrows before nodding toward it. "Do you mind?"

She turned the paper so he could see.

He studied it a moment before asking, "What's your gut feeling about these two women?"

"They were both broken and upset, but not angry. I mean, I'm sure they did feel anger. But I never got vibes from either of them that they were angry at *me*."

"So, you talked to them?"

"I wanted to meet with them. To apologize. Plus, some of the women have done interviews with the media. I told myself not to watch, not to read any of it. But I did anyway. My curiosity got the best of me,

I suppose. I was hoping one of them might say some-thing that would offer some insight as to what was going on in my father's head."

He pulled his phone from his pocket. "Do you mind if I look for some pictures of these women? I'd just like to know what they look like so I can keep my eyes open while we're here on the island."

"That seems like a great idea. Thank you."

He nodded and began typing something into his phone. Olivia glanced at the screen and saw a picture of Starla from one of her social media accounts.

Beautiful Starla.

Her smile seemed to indicate that she'd bounced back from everything that had happened. She had pictures of herself from various vacation spots and surrounded by friends and family.

The next photo was from Nancy's social media.

Nancy didn't look like she'd recovered quite as well. Dark circles hung beneath her eyes and her gaze appeared listless. She'd remarried a thin man with a balding head and a dark mustache. The two of them apparently lived in Utah.

"What's another name?" Anderson asked. "I can write it down for you if it would help."

"I should be able to handle this." Olivia *was* a therapist after all. She was supposed to be able to handle any kind of emotion that came her way. But this situation had put everything to the test—it was just too personal.

She continued to list the other victims that she knew about.

Ann Stafford.

Emily Killinger.

Willa Packard.

Dana Colorado.

When she wrote the last name, she released a long, pent-up breath.

There. She'd done it. She'd listed the people her father had affairs with.

At least, the ones she knew about.

She stared at the names a moment.

Was there a link between any of these women and the woman Olivia had found in the shower? Between any of them and Megan?

Could any of these women be guilty of murder? Olivia didn't want to think that they were. They had already been through enough without Olivia accusing them of sending threatening texts . . . or worse.

Yet, at the same time, she didn't know how she could avoid sharing this information.

She lifted a quick prayer, pleading for wisdom to know if she was doing the right thing.

Anderson finished looking up pictures of all the women and tried to store their images in his mind.

Then he turned back to the list. "Of all the people mentioned, were any of these women especially aggressive toward you?"

Olivia let out a long, almost burdened breath. "If I had to pinpoint anyone it would be Dana Colorado. She actually came to our door screaming at us. Not only did my father have an affair with her, but she also donated to the fake nonprofit he'd started. She demanded her money back. She was the one who kind of unleashed all of this, so to speak."

He found the woman's picture and studied the image of her bright eyes and red hair. "When was the last time you saw her?"

Olivia thought about it a moment before saying, "Probably three weeks ago. She'd been harassing my mother and me, but I've been trying to give her grace, all things considered. But I think she's going to file a civil suit against us. Even though none of the money my father swindled went to our family—our lifestyle was very humble—Dana threatened to come after us for everything."

Anderson leaned back in his seat, trying to comprehend everything Olivia had just told him. He let out a long breath. "So, the incidents that have happened at Dagger Point . . . do any of them involve Megan? Or does it involve one of these women?"

Olivia grimaced. "I don't know. At this point, I guess it could go either way. But I still have no clue who the dead woman in the shower was. Why she was at the house. If her death truly was suicide or if something else happened. Basically, right now, I'm operating on a lack of information. I don't even know where to start."

Anderson leaned toward her, questioning whether he should say these next words or not.

But his gut told him he should.

"I'm not telling you how to proceed," he said. "I'm really not. But if you need my help trying to track down answers, just let me know. I have some experience as a Marine and a firefighter."

Her eyes widened first with what appeared to be surprise and then gratitude. "You would do that for me?"

"This isn't just about you and your family anymore. I was there. I saw the dead bodies. And I'm the one who knew Megan. I don't have as much invested in this as you do, but I do feel invested."

Olivia studied him a moment. "Why did you want to stay at this house specifically?"

He leaned back and let out a long breath. He'd

figured Olivia would get around to asking that question at some point.

He could answer without diving into the details of everything that had happened over the past three months. He wasn't ready to talk about Selena. Not yet.

"My family apparently built the house, and it was my ancestors who died in the original house fire."

"What? I'm so sorry."

"My grandfather told me stories about growing up in the house after it was rebuilt," Anderson started. "He's passed away now. But apparently my family were the first people to own this place. I felt like by coming back here, I would be coming back to my roots. I just feel like I need that right now."

Olivia studied him as if sensing there was more to his story. He was thankful that she didn't ask—but a wave of guilt also swept through him. She'd shared a lot of her story, but he wasn't ready to dive into the details of his past yet.

"I had no idea that this was once your family's place."

"Like I said, I never meant to impose." He shrugged.

"I understand."

He leaned toward her. "How about you and I come up with a plan? See what else we can do to find answers . . . because I'm on the same page as you. I don't have a lot of confidence in the sheriff's department right now. If we're going to be staying at that house, we need to make sure it is safe."

"What kind of plan are you talking about?" Olivia rested her elbows on the table as she waited for him to continue.

"I'm not sure yet. But maybe it should start with talking to Emma Jean tonight at dinner."

Just as he said the words, Olivia's phone buzzed.

She glanced at the screen and her face went pale.

"Olivia?" He watched her carefully.

She held up her phone. "I just got another text. It says: The wicked shall perish. Prepare yourself."

CHAPTER
FIFTEEN

OLIVIA COULDN'T GET the text out of her head. *The wicked shall perish.*

She and Anderson had dropped off her list with Beamer before going back to the house. He'd made a dinner reservation for them, and she had two hours before they needed to leave.

For now, she sat on her bed and closed her eyes to unwind and collect her thoughts for a moment.

The only bright spot to being here on Kiawah Island so far was Anderson. He'd surprised her.

She wasn't looking for a relationship with anyone. But the friendship was nice, as was the nonjudgmental look in his gaze and his steadfast personality.

Still, if she were smart, she'd focus on the tasks at hand—tasks that didn't include Anderson.

She ran through the names of the women her father had affairs with.

Was one of them on the island? Or was it just a coincidence Olivia was receiving these threatening texts and that two dead bodies had turned up?

She had no idea.

She needed to find the money her dad had taken from his victims. The funds weren't in any of his bank accounts. Olivia had checked. It appeared he'd cleaned out three secret online accounts, including one offshore account.

And if he'd cashed them out, that meant that he'd put the money somewhere.

Somewhere no one would think to look.

A secret house seemed like the best option.

However, it was a possibility that he could have other secret homes as well. Maybe he'd set up shell organizations that paid for them.

Maybe he had multiple houses he could hide money in.

There was so much she didn't know.

He must have known someone was going to rat him out about what he was doing. He must have been desperate to close his accounts.

If Olivia could find that money, she had every intention of paying it back to his victims.

The problem was, where would he leave it in a place like this?

She'd already done a preliminary search of all the obvious places. Closets and drawers and under beds. Behind picture frames and inside air duct vents.

But she had known that would be too easy.

So where else did that leave?

And if the money wasn't here, where would it be?

Olivia needed closure. The one thing she could think of to give her that very closure was repaying this money. She would repay it out of her own pocket if she could, but she didn't have those kinds of funds.

She didn't have three million dollars.

Disgust roiled inside her. She still couldn't believe that her father had done these things. Her father—the man she'd looked up to so very much. For years, she'd practically thought he walked on water. She hadn't been the only one. So many of his followers had him up on a pedestal.

Once, several years ago, someone had hinted to Olivia that her dad had less than honorable intentions. But she brushed the allegation off, figuring that speculation just came with popularity.

Little had she known that those words were the truth. She'd had blinders on.

If she had listened to them, maybe she wouldn't

be in this situation right now. Guilt had haunted her ever since she found out the truth.

She should have at least considered the possibility.

She should have been a better listener.

Her shoulders slumped.

Her phone rang, and she saw it was her brother, Rex. He was a cop now living in Minnesota. He'd wanted to put as much distance between himself and their father's notoriety as possible. He'd even stopped going to church—maybe even stopped believing in God all together.

Her heart hurt for the situation.

She quickly answered. "Hey, you."

"Hey, sis. How's it going?"

She glanced around her room. "It's going."

"Did you go to Kiawah?"

She swallowed hard. Her brother had told her not to come. "I did."

"Find any answers?"

"No, but I want to make things right."

"You're not the one who messed up."

"I know." She pressed her eyes shut, wishing her life hadn't turned into such a nightmare.

"Don't you have to work?"

"They canned me." As soon as the news had broken about what had happened, the station that hosted her radio show had come up with an excuse to let her go. She'd lost her book deal. Even her friends had walked away.

"What? You didn't tell me that."

She pulled her knees to her chest. "No one wants to be associated with our family right now."

"I know." He sobered. "What can I do?"

"Nothing. I'm just trying to figure things out here."

"Be careful, okay?"

She'd told him about some of those text messages. He'd tried to trace them but couldn't.

She considered telling him about the dead body.

But she wouldn't. Not now, at least.

She also thought about mentioning Anderson, thought about asking her brother to run a background check on him.

She didn't do that either. Mostly because she wouldn't want someone doing that to her.

Either way, it felt good to talk to Rex. To talk to someone who understood her pain.

She missed her brother. She missed the way things used to be, back when she had her blinders on. She knew there was no going back. Her life would never be the same again, and she couldn't pretend like it would.

As she ended the call, she stared at her phone and remembered those texts.

If the person who sent these messages was the same person who was behind any of the recent incidents, that would mean this person was also on the island.

That they were stuck here, along with the other residents.

That realization made Olivia want to throw up.

She had no idea how things were going to play out while she was on the island.

But she knew there was potential for a disaster.

And she had no way to escape.

Anderson decided to get his jog in before dinner. It would help him to burn off some steam.

But as his feet hit the sand near the shoreline, all he could think about was spotting Megan washed up on the beach, rolling in and out with the waves.

What had happened to her?

He could ask the sheriff's office, but he doubted they'd share.

He only knew that a bad feeling swirled in his gut.

He'd been in a lot of dangerous situations before

as a firefighter. Had risked his safety many times. He'd almost lost his life twice.

But God had somehow seen to it that Anderson had survived.

Unfortunately, he couldn't say the same for Selena.

Selena's death had turned his life upside down in so many ways.

It had shown him new sides of the people around him. Sides he didn't like.

He'd taken a leave of absence from his job. The fire chief had told him to take as much time as necessary.

That's exactly what Anderson had intended on doing. That's why he had rented this place for a month.

He was clearly going to have to change those plans, especially now that he knew Megan had ulterior motives about renting this place.

But was that really what the woman was doing? Did she have some kind of side business going on?

What if she was just going to pocket the money he'd paid and keep it for herself?

Maybe she'd been running some kind of scam all over the island and that was why she'd been killed.

Then there was the woman in the shower . . . had she been murdered? And if so, had the person responsible for her death known some type of evidence was on that footage Megan had obtained? Would they have killed Megan in order to keep that information from getting into the hands of law enforcement?

Anderson wasn't sure, but he needed to consider the possibility.

Something strange was going on at this house. No one could deny that.

All he wanted was to explore his heritage and regroup here at the house. But that didn't seem like a possibility. Not right now.

As soon as the bridge opened, he needed to find a different house in a different location. Although Olivia offered to let him stay here with her, she didn't deserve to be put out.

Maybe—just maybe—he could talk Olivia into letting him rent this place after she went back home.

He hoped that tonight at dinner she would be able to speak with Emma Jean and find some answers.

Although, if Anderson was wise, he'd simply stay to himself while he was here on the island.

He finished his jog and started back to the house.

He had just enough time to shower and get cleaned up. He looked forward to getting to know Olivia more. It wasn't a date—or anything like that.

But he was curious about the woman, and this would be a good chance to learn more.

Plus, he couldn't deny that there was something about her that intrigued him—and it was more than her good looks. She had a depth of character that he didn't often encounter.

He paused on the walkover and sucked in a few deep breaths.

As he did, a shadow moved behind some trees in the distance.

Was someone watching him?

He didn't know.

But he didn't like the possibility. Not with every-thing that had been happening.

He broke into a jog again, suddenly feeling the urge to make sure Olivia was safe.

OLIVIA WASN'T sure what to wear for dinner tonight. She didn't want to be too dressed up and make it seem like this was a big deal. Nor did she want to look like a bum.

She settled on a pale pink sundress and some strappy sandals.

She didn't know why she felt nervous. But she couldn't ignore the fact that butterflies played in her stomach.

Not because she was attracted to Anderson.

Even though she *was* attracted to him.

However, she wasn't looking for romance. This dinner was simply a way for him to say thank you, to distract her from the worries plaguing her, and mostly to talk to Emma Jean.

Her breath caught when she met Anderson

outside precisely at six and saw him in his sky-blue T-shirt and khaki shorts. He really did clean up nicely. She'd known he was handsome. But something about him right now made him look exceptionally handsome.

Olivia had to admit that she was curious about his story.

Why was he really here? She'd seen the distracted look in his gaze and knew there was more to his coming to the island.

Maybe she would find out tonight.

Or, if she was smart, she'd keep the conversation away from the personal.

"You look nice." He cast an approving glance. "Thank you again for joining me."

"Thank you for the invitation. I've been craving some good crab cakes."

"I hear this restaurant has the best. I looked up some reviews before I came."

He helped her into his truck before he climbed behind the steering wheel, and they took off down the road.

Several minutes later, Olivia and Anderson pulled up to a restaurant situated near the northern tip of the island.

They were seated on an open porch with grand columns, elegant tables, and sweeping views of the ocean, marsh, and a top-notch golf course. The view was truly unmatched.

Olivia glanced around, searching for trouble. But no one appeared to be watching her.

Not yet, at least.

Now she needed to figure out who Emma Jean was.

After the waitress took their orders, they both leaned back in their chairs, a gentle breeze washing over them.

She glanced around the restaurant and saw the other diners, each looking elegant in their expensive clothing and with their refined manners. A honey-blonde with a dour look on her face as she stared at the golf course. A family of four who bickered over who got the last hushpuppy. A young couple who smiled softly at each other.

Olivia scanned the waitresses, but none of their nametags read Emma Jean.

Perhaps the woman had taken off work today. Perhaps she was in mourning over her friend.

All of this could be for nothing.

"What are you thinking?"

Anderson's voice pulled her from her thoughts. She glanced at his inquisitive face and shrugged. "I'm a bit overwhelmed, to tell the truth."

"I can only imagine."

"I'm not one who usually plays detective. How about you?"

He rocked his head back and forth with thought. "I can't say I do. I do have some experience with fire investigations, I suppose. But I usually just try to save people."

"Like you're saving me now?" She flashed an almost weak smile.

"I don't know if I'd say that."

"My brother is a cop," she told him. "He always said firefighters were the ones who got all the glory, who could do no wrong. And the police were the ones who put themselves in danger every day and were hated for it."

"I don't know about that. But if he feels that way, it sounds like he should have become a firefighter."

She let out a chuckle. "Maybe."

The waitress delivered their appetizer—crab dip —and Anderson said a quick prayer before they both grabbed tortilla chips and dug in.

The dip was delicious, the perfect balance of creaminess and spice.

"Tell me what you do." Anderson held a chip in his hands.

That seemed like a safe enough subject. She told him about her ministry to ministers, and he listened attentively as she spoke, not looking bored at all.

"That's really great what you're doing. I had a cousin in ministry. He lasted six years, and now he works at a used car lot. He said he couldn't handle the pressure."

"You'd be surprised at how many feel that way. I honestly love what I do. But I'm on hiatus for now. I've got to get my own life straight before I can try to get other people's lives straightened out."

"That makes sense."

She glanced across the table at Anderson, wondering if he would open up.

Because she sensed he was also hiding secrets.

Olivia looked at Anderson with curiosity in her gaze.

He really didn't want to talk about his past. But he felt as if he should share more about himself.

However, his life was multifaceted. Where should he even begin?

"So, I already told you my family used to own Seacret Hideout. I'm talking about a hundred years ago. I've always wanted to come here and see it."

"So, you've never been to this island before?"

He shook his head. "No, I haven't. But my grandfather told me stories about living here as a child. I was fascinated by what he said, and I knew I had to see it for myself."

"That's good that you can get back to your roots."

Even though Olivia said the words, Anderson saw she still had unanswered questions. Like, how did someone in the prime of his career manage to take off a month of work to come here?

Anderson picked up another chip and broke it in half as his thoughts churned inside him.

"Another reason I came here is because there was a fire, and my ex-fiancée was killed in it. I wasn't able to save her. To say that that's affected me would be an understatement." Anderson's voice cracked under the strain of his words.

There was much more to that story also, but he felt like this simplified version would do for now.

Olivia reached across the table and quickly squeezed his hand before releasing it. "I'm so sorry to hear that. I can only imagine."

"It's been tough, to say the least. I guess I'm still trying to figure out how to rebuild after that happened."

"I can understand that also. It sounds like we're both trying to rebuild our lives. I found out some things about my father that really turned my life upside down."

His curiosity grew. He wanted to know more, but he knew it wasn't his place to ask.

As he glanced outside at the beach, he spotted a man half hidden behind the dunes.

Was this the same guy he'd seen before?

He wasn't sure.

But this one held a camera.

Instantly, his spine stiffened.

That camera was aimed at them.

He was sure of it.

"Anderson?"

"Excuse me a minute." He rose from his seat and started toward the steps leading to the ocean.

As he did, the man with the camera took off into a run heading for the parking lot.

And Anderson took off after him.

OLIVIA FOLLOWED Anderson with her gaze.

That's when she saw the man running from the dunes.

With a camera.

Had he been taking pictures of them?

Her heart raced faster.

Several other patrons in the restaurant seemed to notice what was happening and turned to watch Anderson chase the man.

But the man with the camera had too much of a head start.

He ran straight toward the parking lot. A moment later, Olivia heard a car start and then squeal out of the lot.

He'd gotten away, hadn't he?

A few minutes later, Anderson reappeared.

Despite the way he gulped air as if out of breath, his gaze was still hard.

"He was taking pictures of us," Anderson said as he lowered himself back at the table. "And I wanted to know why."

Olivia's heart pounded into her chest.

"If this guy is on the island, then he's going to be here until the bridge opens," Olivia reminded him. "Maybe we'll run into him."

Anderson's gaze met hers. "Why would someone be taking pictures of us?"

Olivia swallowed hard.

This was it. It was her invitation to share more details about what was going on.

But did she want to do that?

Or did she want to keep them to herself?

If there was one thing she'd learned through her father it was that there was value in being authentic, that secrets could harm more than they could help.

She was trying to rid herself of the shame she felt because of her father's actions.

But maybe the first step in overcoming that would be to speak freely about her life over the past six months.

Anderson knew he probably shouldn't have asked the question. But the fact somebody was taking pictures of Olivia set off all kinds of alarms in his head.

Or were they taking pictures of *him*?

What had happened with Selena had been tragic, and her friends blamed him for her death.

But would someone go as far as to follow him here and take pictures?

It didn't seem likely. Why would they even want to?

Anderson had no idea. But he needed to remain on guard until he knew what was going on.

Before they could talk more, their food was delivered. Her crab cakes looked—and smelled—scrumptious. Old Bay mingled with onion from her salad and the aroma of freshly baked bread.

Olivia picked up her fork and began picking at her crab cake before saying, "My father was Larry Beaumont."

He paused. That name sounded familiar.

Then it hit him.

Anderson had heard of him before. His story had been on the news. In magazine articles.

What he'd done had caused quite a stir.

He realized Olivia was waiting for his response, and he nodded.

"I didn't realize that . . ." he finally said.

"He was called America's pastor for a long time. He led a church of ten thousand people. He had a radio program. Book deals. Conferences. The whole works."

"It's all coming back to me now."

"Ever since the scandal broke, most of my friends either abandoned me or they only talked to me about it because they wanted some juicy gossip. It's been a lot to process. I think I've internalized far too much."

"That sounds really tough to deal with."

"It has been." Olivia let out a breath. "The truth is not only was my father inappropriate with some of the women, but he also stole money he'd designated for a nonprofit. It disappeared and no one knows what happened to it."

"You mentioned before there was some money involved."

"But what I didn't tell you was that it's three million dollars," she admitted.

His eyes widened. "That's a lot of cash."

She nodded. "Yes, it is. After his death, a lot of people turned their vengeance about the situation onto my family. There's been a lot of hate mail and even some death threats. I lost my job. And I lost my fiancé."

"Hard times will definitely show you who your true friends are."

"Absolutely." She played with her straw. "You speak about it as if you know."

"I do."

She shrugged and continued. "I thought if I came here, maybe I could get some answers. My father killed himself, and I didn't find out about the house until after he died."

"If you don't mind me asking—how did everything come out in the open?"

"One of the women came forward and shared her story with a local newspaper, and it went national. Then more women came forward."

"How did your father react?"

"At first, he denied it. We all did. I stood behind him—publicly. But as more women came forward, I couldn't deny it anymore. I confronted my dad about it and asked him point-blank to tell me the truth. And he did. He owned up to everything. Broke down in tears. Pleaded for forgiveness."

"But he didn't explain himself?"

"He said there was no excuse. Then the church fired him and, without saying anything else, he withdrew. He used his friend's rental home to get away from the media scrutiny, to take some time to figure things out. But . . ." Her voice cracked.

"You don't have to finish."

"It's okay. I want to. He took his own life. He overdosed on some anxiety medication the doctor had given him. For a moment, I both hated him and felt guilty for not trying to save him. I should have done more. I just never thought . . ." She couldn't finish.

"I can only imagine how complex the situation was."

She drew in a deep breath to compose herself. "Anyway, I still want to know why he conned those women. Why our family and his ministry weren't enough. Why he felt the need to go beyond everything he already had and touch that forbidden fruit."

"I hate to say it, but there's probably a little bit of that rebellion in all of us—a little bit of the desire for forbidden fruit. It goes all the way back to Adam and Eve."

Olivia couldn't deny his words. "I know. But the authorities haven't been able to find this money he had. I figured that the least I could do was to look for it and give it back to the victims. I would pay it back out of my own pocket if I could. But I don't have that kind of cash. However, I thought maybe I could sell this house. That I could liquidate some things and see what I could do."

He leaned closer. "This sounds like a lot of burden that you're taking on because of your father."

She shrugged, suddenly feeling weighed down. "It has been difficult. And people haven't been kind. I wanted to get away where no one recognizes me. I figured if I came here, I could hide out and look for the money . . ."

As Olivia glanced across the restaurant, a waitress who'd just come on duty caught her eye.

She appeared to be the same age as Megan with dark, curly hair that was cut to her chin.

Olivia strained to see the woman's name tag from where she sat.

"You think that's Emma Jean?" Anderson followed her gaze.

"I think it's a good possibility."

"Then we need to figure out how to talk to her." Anderson glanced around. "We could be sneaky, or we could simply be direct."

"How about a mix of both?"

When the waitress came back to refill their drinks, Anderson pointed at the new waitress. "Excuse me, but the woman over there looks familiar. Could you tell me her name?"

The waitress followed his gaze and turned back to them. "Oh, that's Emma Jean. She's a staple around here. All her customers love her and request to be seated at her tables. She's kind of my hero."

"Maybe she served me last time I was here too," Anderson said. "And I'm pretty sure she made a recommendation of her favorite dessert. I'm having trouble remembering what it is though. Is there any chance you could ask her if she could come over this way?"

"Sure, I would be more than happy to."

The waitress disappeared, and a moment later, Emma Jean stood by their table. Her eyes looked dull, as if she'd been crying but was trying to hold herself together. "I hear you're a past customer?"

"The truth is I've never been here before," Anderson started. "But we were hoping to ask you some questions."

Her smile slipped, and she stepped back. "Are you guys cops or something?"

"No, but we knew Megan," Olivia said.

Her gaze flittered back and forth between the two of them. "How? I don't remember seeing either of you around here before. This is a small island."

"We're staying at the house on Dagger Point," Olivia said. "Megan was found nearby. She was supposed to stop by that morning."

Realization swept through Emma Jean's gaze

before her spine seemed to stiffen. "What do you want to know about her?"

Olivia cleared her throat before starting. "We're trying to figure out what happened to her. You've probably heard that there was a dead body found beneath the house before Megan passed."

Emma Jean's frown deepened. "It's been the talk of the island, to say the least. That and the bridge. Everyone's kind of spooked over it all, to be honest."

"Anyone in their right mind would feel a little off-balance considering we're stuck on the island with two dead bodies." Olivia kept her voice soft and compassionate. "Unfortunately, Megan had some answers that I need, but I didn't have a chance to ask her. I was hoping you might know something."

Emma Jean glanced around as if to see if anyone was listening.

"I don't know what kind of information I could tell you. Megan was a great woman, and I'm going to miss her terribly." Tears gleamed in her gaze.

"I'm sorry," Olivia said. "I don't mean to upset you. I really don't. I wouldn't be talking to you right now if it wasn't important. Was Megan in trouble?"

Olivia halfway expected an immediate "no." But, instead, Emma Jean paused for a moment. "I don't know. Megan hadn't been acting like herself in recent months, but she wouldn't tell me why."

"Do you have any guesses?" Anderson leaned toward Emma Jean.

Emma Jean glanced around again. "Look, I can't talk right now. I have to get to work. But no, I don't know for sure exactly what was going on. I only know she wasn't entirely acting like herself. She almost seemed preoccupied."

"Was she having money problems?" Olivia asked.

"Not that I know of. But she probably wouldn't tell me if she did. Sure, we were friends. But Megan was the type who liked to appear to have it all together, even around her friends."

"But she didn't have it all together?" Olivia clarified.

"Who does?" Emma Jean sighed. "Listen, I'm not sure exactly where she stood financially."

"Was there anything she said that might hint as to what was going on?" Anderson asked. "I know you need to get going. But if you could just tell me . . ."

"All I know is that she mentioned some guy named Abraham. I don't know who he is. I don't even have a last name. And I've never met anybody on the island with that name. That's all I know." She shrugged and took a step away as if losing patience.

"One last question before you go." Olivia kept her voice soft. "Is there any way that we could get into Megan's house or apartment or wherever she was living and take a look around? Like I said, I needed to ask her some questions, but I didn't have the chance to."

Emma Jean's brow furrowed. "Questions about what?"

"About what was going on at my property."

"I'm sorry." She stepped back. "I can't help you."

"Here's my number if you think of something that might be important." Olivia handed her a business card with her new phone number scrawled on the front. "Call me anytime."

With that, Emma Jean nodded and hurried away.

"She definitely knows more than she's letting on," Anderson said as he followed Emma Jean with his gaze.

"I agree. There's more to this story. But I don't think she's going to open up now. Maybe we should give her a little time."

He turned his thoughts over in his mind for a moment as he stared at the beach in the distance and the muted colors of the sunset. "I like the idea of getting into Megan's apartment. If Megan was doing some type of secret deal, she probably had records of it somewhere. But I don't know how we can get permission to look around."

"No doubt sheriff deputies have already looked inside." Olivia ran her finger down the edge of her sweaty glass of water. "But I'm not hopeful they'll share anything with us."

Anderson stared at her a moment. "If you do somehow get a chance to look around her apartment, what exactly are you hoping to find?"

"I'm trying to figure out how the bills at this house were being paid. My father passed away six months ago. I haven't made a single payment to this place. Not a mortgage payment. Not an electric or water bill. So how is it being paid?"

"Maybe you could contact the bank to find out."

"That's the thing." Olivia shrugged. "My mom and I tried. There are no records of these bills in my father's checking account. If anyone knew the answers to that question, I thought it could have been Megan."

"You might be right. I feel certain she was doing something below board. We just need to figure out what. And I'm not sure if Emma Jean will share anything else with us."

"In the meantime, we should keep our eyes open for some guy named Abraham. But I'm not hopeful he's simply going to stumble into our laps."

"I agree." Anderson let out a breath before pulling out his card and paying the bill. It was getting late, and they'd had a long day. He knew they could both use some rest.

Twilight had already fallen outside, and he thought getting some sleep might be the best thing for both him and Olivia.

Maybe in the morning, they'd be able to think a little more clearly and find some of the answers they both so desperately desired.

Or more danger could be waiting.

He didn't consider himself a pessimist or a betting man. But if he were—his bets would be on danger.

OLIVIA AWOKE the next morning to the sound of her phone ringing.

She sat up in bed and grabbed it, thrusting the device to her ear before she even looked at the caller ID. "Hello?"

"Sorry to call you so early," a slow voice drawled. "It's Deputy Beamer. I have an update I wanted to talk to you about."

Olivia was instantly awake. "I'm listening."

"We have an ID on the victim found in the shower beneath your house. Her name is Kasey Winthrop. Does that sound familiar?"

Olivia sat with the name a moment before finally saying, "No. I'm sorry, but it doesn't ring any bells. Can you tell me anything else about her?"

"She's from Charleston. A bit of a nomad with no

real career, so to speak. Her last job was working as a clerk in a department store. But she left that job about six months ago."

Six months ago? That was when her father had died. Was that a coincidence?

Olivia had no idea. But she needed more information. She had to find out what Beamer might share with her.

"What about cause of death?" Olivia asked, pulling her knees to her chest.

"It's still undetermined." Beamer didn't sound quite as icy right now as he had yesterday—but he still didn't sound exactly friendly either. "Pinpointing what happened to her could prove to be difficult."

"What about Megan?" Olivia continued, knowing she might be pressing her luck. "Do you have a cause of death for her?"

"We managed to get the coroner here via boat. He believes the primary cause of death is drowning. But the question of what happened to her before she drowned remains."

Something had *definitely* happened to Megan before she went into that water. "Were there bruises? Any signs of a struggle?"

"There you go being that armchair detective again." He let out a sigh. "She had several bruises. We're not sure if the bruises were from a fight or from a fall. But I assure you that we're investigating. If you remember anything else about her, let me know."

"Will do."

Olivia ended the call, and her thoughts raced.

Kasey Winthrop.

The name didn't sound familiar—not at all.

Olivia had some research to do to see if she could find any connections between Kasey and her father.

As Anderson drank some coffee, his phone buzzed. He looked down and saw he'd received a text message from Olivia. They'd exchanged numbers last night.

Are you awake? Can I come down?

His curiosity rose. If Olivia was texting him this early, she probably had a good reason for it.

He quickly responded before striding across the room and unlocking the door.

Olivia rushed downstairs a moment later, a laptop

tucked beneath her arm and her eyes dancing with excitement. "Deputy Beamer called me."

"Did he have an update?"

She quickly filled him in. As she talked, she sat down at the small dinette. Anderson poured her a cup of coffee as he listened.

"Kasey Winthrop? That name doesn't sound familiar to me either."

"I'm going to do some research. But I wanted to share that update with you first." Olivia paused and took a sip of her coffee. "You fixed this perfectly. Thank you."

"I aim to please."

She flashed him a look that he couldn't read. Maybe it was amusement. Maybe it was surprise. He wasn't sure.

She began typing on her laptop. Anderson scooted his chair closer so he could see better.

As he did, the sweet smell of daisies rose up around him. The scent was pleasant and simple.

But Anderson couldn't dwell on that right now. This wasn't the time or place.

After Olivia typed in Kasey's name, they sorted through several results until they found a picture of the woman. She looked beautiful and vibrant with her dark hair and dancing eyes—quite the contrast to how they'd found her.

Things could change in an instant. He knew that better than anyone.

They scrolled through her social media pages, looking for anything that might catch their eye.

Finally, after they'd looked for at least thirty minutes, Olivia paused on a picture.

"I've seen this woman somewhere before." Olivia pointed to a photo of a twenty-something woman with light-brown hair, a thin face, and a colorful cloth headband across her forehead.

Realization filled Anderson. "She was at the restaurant last night."

Olivia sucked in a breath. "You're right. If we can find her, maybe we can find out more information about Kasey."

He tilted his head. "It sounds like you're all in with looking into this."

"This isn't normally my thing. It's not what I do. But I have to have answers. I have to know if this woman is somehow connected with my father. Megan as well. I can't just sit back and pretend like none of this happened."

"Then let me be your sidekick."

She stared at him a moment. "You mean that?"

"Of course. Besides, you don't have a car to use right now. Even though part of this island is walkable, it's going to take you a lot longer to find answers on foot."

Olivia stared at him another moment before nodding. "Okay then. I'll take you up on that offer. But only if I'm not pulling you away from something else."

Was she pulling him away from anything else? Not really. Anderson had wanted to dig into his family's history, but that could wait. This seemed more urgent—although another part of Anderson thought that this was a terrible idea.

Minding their own business seemed to be the best option.

But Olivia didn't seem to be open to that.

Anderson understood where she was coming from. The need to find answers felt dire, especially in the wake of everything else that happened.

"Just let me know what you need, and I'll be there."

CHAPTER
NINETEEN

OLIVIA THOUGHT she'd feel better knowing Anderson had agreed to help.

But his involvement only seemed to up the stakes.

They'd agreed they wouldn't find any answers by staying in the house today, and Olivia had no illusions of sitting on the beach and relaxing—not on this trip, at least.

So that meant they'd need to get out and about, to mingle with people, talk to them, see if anyone else had any insight.

They agreed to meet outside, but Olivia stepped out and noted that Anderson wasn't there yet.

As she waited for him, she glanced at her car and frowned. Those slashed tires were a reminder that someone was desperate to silence her, to deter her, to let her know she was in the line of fire.

She averted her gaze to the house on the right.

An older man stood between the trees watching her. He was balding and thin with drawn features and a stooped back.

She froze, wondering if his intentions were nefarious. Then she realized he was pruning a tree.

Was he her neighbor?

Maybe she should find out.

Gathering her courage, she strode toward him. "Good morning."

"Morning." He continued clipping limbs.

"I'm Olivia."

"Frank. I'm trying to clean up these mulberry trees. I don't know why the song calls them bushes— all around the mulberry bush. You remember that one? Anyway, these berries get everywhere. The birds love them, though. I for one am tired of them pooping these berries all over my car."

"I can imagine . . ."

He glanced at her again, his gaze cautious. "I know who your father was."

She swallowed, trying not to let her stress get the best of her. "Larry Beaumont. Did you ever see him here?"

"I did. There were usually two cars. His, then a day or so later another car would pull up. After they went inside, they hardly ever came out. I always wondered what was going on in there."

Olivia swallowed, hating hearing about what her father was doing. Hating picturing him in the middle of his scam. But she had to face the truth.

"Did you ever hear or see anything unusual?"

"Like I said, once they went inside, I hardly ever saw them again. Except once."

Oliva stepped closer, her curiosity officially pricked. "What happened that time?"

Anderson stepped outside and joined her, quietly listening.

"He was having an argument with someone." The man shrugged as he squeezed his pruning shears together. "A very heated argument from the sounds of it."

Olivia's lungs seemed to freeze. "Could you hear what it was about?"

"Not really. But I heard something crash. Thought maybe they were throwing things at each other."

Throwing things? That didn't sound like her dad.

Then again . . . what did she know?

"Did you call the cops?" Olivia asked.

Frank shrugged, his gaze not leaving the bush he was working on. "No, figured it was none of my business."

"Did you get a good look at the woman he was with when that happened?" Anderson asked.

"Good look? I wouldn't say that. But I did see her leaving the next morning."

Olivia's pulse continued to thrum in her ears. "Could you describe her?"

"She was probably in her thirties. Skinny. Pretty. And she had red hair."

"There's only one person on that list I made who has red hair," Olivia told Anderson as they climbed into his truck. "Dana Colorado."

He glanced at her as he cranked the engine. "What do you think she and your father were arguing about?"

Olivia thought about it a moment before shrugging, almost in frustration. "Maybe she discovered my dad wasn't who he claimed to be. Or maybe he asked for money. Maybe she even gave him money and then demanded it back. There are so many possibilities."

"Maybe she's where you need to focus next."

He was right. But there was one other thing bothering her.

Olivia turned toward Anderson. "Whoever is

responsible should be on this island right now. That's what perplexes me. If this somehow centers around me, then someone either knew I was coming here or they followed me. But if housing is as tight as Megan said it is, then they'd have nowhere to stay."

Anderson studied her face, his gaze shadowed with thought. "Did you tell anyone before you came?"

"Only one friend. She wouldn't say anything. She knows I didn't want the media to catch wind and look for trouble."

He rubbed a hand over his face. "If Kasey was dead before you came, then the connection seems doubtful."

"What if my dad had more going on than bringing women here? More than conning people out of money? What if he had some kind of side hustle going on?" She almost didn't want to say it. She didn't want this to be any worse than it had to be. But she couldn't deny the possibilities either.

Anderson let out a skeptical grunt before shaking his head. "That seems unlikely. He was a predator, but not *that* kind of predator."

Olivia sighed and crossed her arms over her chest, unable to deny his words. "You're right. I just can't put the pieces together."

"Be patient."

"I'm trying. Believe me, I am. But I so desperately want to put this behind me. It doesn't seem like I can do that until I have answers."

"Then we'll keep looking. Step by step."

As the words left Anderson's mouth, Olivia's phone rang again.

She didn't recognize the number, but the area code was local.

After a moment of hesitation, she decided to answer.

OLIVIA PUT the phone to her ear. "Hello?"

"Olivia? It's me. Emma Jean," she whispered. "I've been thinking about our conversation. I need to know what happened to Megan also. I don't know if you and your boyfriend are the ones who will figure it out, but I trust you more than I do Beamer and Clinton."

"I appreciate the vote of confidence . . ."

"The keycode to get into Megan's place is 91682." She rattled off the address to a riverside condo. "I'm pretty sure the sheriff has already been inside, but maybe you'll find something he didn't. However, if anyone asks me, I don't know anything about this."

"Got it. Thank you so much."

Olivia ended the call and turned to Anderson, sharing the update with him.

"Is that where you want to go now?" He shifted.

She nodded. "It is. But I understand if you don't want to go with me."

"It's not a problem."

She stared at him a moment. "Are you sure?"

"Positive. You need someone watching your back. I'm your sidekick, remember? Where you go, I go."

"But if you're caught . . ." The last thing she wanted was to get him in trouble, especially since he was an innocent bystander here.

His gaze locked onto hers. "If I'm caught, I'll be fine. My life is already on the rocks right now. This won't change that."

On the rocks? There was clearly more to his story.

But Olivia would worry about that later.

Right now, she wanted to get to Megan's place and see if she could find any answers.

Anderson didn't like this, but he knew he couldn't stop Olivia from going to Megan's place. So, he might as well join her in case she ran into trouble.

Following her directions, he pulled up to a small building that looked to house six condos.

Before getting out of the truck, Anderson turned to her one more time. "You sure about this?"

Olivia stared at the building a moment before nodding. "I am. I need to know what's going on."

Anderson nodded, not asking her any more questions. He'd wanted to give her one last opportunity to get out of this before they put her plan into motion.

As they climbed out of his truck, he glanced around.

He didn't see anyone nearby watching.

Quickly, they climbed the stairs to the second floor. Olivia punched in the code to the door, and the electronic lock turned.

This was it. No going back now.

Olivia hesitated only a moment before stepping inside.

Anderson quickly followed behind her and shut the door just in case anyone was watching.

Standing just inside the entry, he scanned the place.

It looked like somewhere he'd expect Megan to live. Everything was neat and well decorated as if it had been staged for sale.

But things weren't always as they seemed on the surface.

Was Megan up to something? Or had she just been in the wrong place at the wrong time?

That's what they needed to find answers to.

CHAPTER
TWENTY-ONE

OLIVIA STARED around the condo a moment, noting the pleasant scent of clean cotton and expensive perfume.

Megan had a casual taste with a white slip-covered sofa and chairs. Three colorful poofs that could be used as footstools or seats were scattered around the space, and live plants added warmth to the room.

Megan would never enjoy this place again, and that seemed like a shame.

At least, maybe the person who'd taken her life would pay.

Olivia sucked in a breath. "Why don't we split up so we can make better use of our time?"

"Sounds like a good idea. Why don't you search

the living room, and I'll head back toward the bedroom?"

"Sounds good."

Olivia watched Anderson disappear down the hallway before heading toward the end tables. She opened the drawers there and searched through them, but all she found were some user manuals, remotes, and a couple of old magazines.

There was a stack of real estate papers, all million-dollar houses that were for sale. Some were on the island and others were in the surrounding area. Seemed typical that a real estate agent would have something like this here.

She searched the contents atop the coffee table but there was nothing there either.

Next, she moved to a buffet across the room and started through those drawers. But it was mostly dinnerware, plates, and placemats.

Her gaze stopped on a picture.

She picked it up and studied it a moment.

It was a photo of Megan with a man who appeared to be around the same age. The guy had dark hair and wore a backward baseball cap, an old T-shirt, and ratty jean shorts. The photo appeared to be taken at a beach in the Caribbean, based on the turquoise water behind them and the palm trees.

Was this guy Abraham? She pulled out her phone and took a quick picture of the image for reference.

Knowing she couldn't waste any more time, Olivia moved into the kitchen and began to search there.

But there was nothing.

She sagged against the counter as more disappointment bit at her.

"Hey, Olivia! Come see this."

Her spirits lifted. Maybe Anderson had found something.

She hurried down a short hallway and into a bedroom to the left—the master suite.

Anderson stood beside a small desk there holding a paper in his hands.

"Any idea what this might mean?" He showed the paper to her.

She studied the letters and numbers written there. But they didn't make sense.

ND 32 -81 6/12

AM 35 -75 6/24

BW 29 -81 6/29

The list went on and on, at least ten more lines.

"These aren't phone numbers or social security numbers. I'm not sure what these mean." Olivia took out her phone and took a photo of it also, just in case.

"It might not have anything to do with what

happened." Anderson's gaze remained on the paper, and he narrowed his eyes with thought. "Or it could have everything to do with this."

"I agree." She stared at it another moment, wishing something would click in her mind.

"Did you find anything?" He turned to her.

Her breath caught. She was entirely closer to Anderson than she'd realized.

Olivia shook her head. "Only a photo of Megan with a man. I have no idea if it means anything or not."

Before they could talk any longer, a noise filled the air.

It was the front door.

Opening.

Someone was coming inside this condo.

Anderson grabbed Olivia's arm and opened the louvered closet door. Quickly, he pulled her inside, slipping in behind her and shutting the door.

As faint wisps of light drifted through the slats, he put his finger over his lips motioning for her to be quiet.

For all they knew, a killer could be coming into the house right now.

Or the sheriff.

Either way, the two of them didn't want to be caught trespassing.

Instead, they stood stiffly and waited.

Anderson was keenly aware of how close they were standing in the confined space. He caught another whiff of Olivia's daisy-scented perfume. The smell was surprisingly tantalizing.

He had the urge to reach out and touch her. To put his hand on her back to try to calm her.

But he didn't. He didn't know Olivia well enough to offer that kind of reassurance.

Instead, his heart pounded in his ears as he waited.

He heard a door close. Heard footsteps.

If he had to guess, the person was going into the kitchen.

Something opened. Maybe the refrigerator or a cabinet?

More silence passed. He and Olivia simply stood there.

Olivia glanced up at him, worry creasing the skin between her eyes.

What Anderson wouldn't do just to be able to reach up and try to soothe some of that anxiety.

He didn't expect to feel so protective of this woman he hardly knew. But from the time they'd first met, he had. It wasn't because he felt like Olivia needed protecting. It wasn't because she was weak.

Something about the vulnerable look in her eyes called to him.

"Just stay still," he whispered.

She nodded, not arguing with him.

His lungs stiffened as the footsteps began to move again.

The person inside the condo was coming closer. Closer.

Then a shadow moved into the room.

Whoever was here was only mere feet away from them.

Anderson didn't know who this person was, but he felt certain he wasn't a cop.

CHAPTER
TWENTY-TWO

OLIVIA FELT her heart pounding in her chest.

Who would come into the apartment?

And her even bigger concern: was this someone who was welcome or someone who was snooping just like Olivia and Anderson were?

She was all too aware of Anderson standing beside her. All too aware of his stiff muscles. All too aware of the lingering scent of his sage-infused cologne.

She resisted the urge to lean on him, to relish his protectiveness.

She'd be out of line to do that right now, no matter what her instincts told her.

As the person paced farther into the room, she squinted.

If she tried hard enough, she could barely make out his outline through the slits.

It was definitely a man. Wearing black.

But he wasn't the same man from the photo. This was someone different.

And if she had to guess, he was looking for something.

She watched, hoping that maybe a new clue would be revealed.

The man didn't particularly seem like someone looking to enjoy the beach—not wearing his black pants and black T-shirt. She couldn't see his face that well. He wore a hat, but shaggy blond hair peeked out from the edges.

Olivia froze when she realized he was going through Megan's room drawer by drawer.

He was looking for something.

What if he opened this closet door in the process?

She was nearly certain she'd seen something glimmer near his belt.

A gun?

That was Olivia's best guess.

He strode away from the nightstand and headed toward the closet.

Instinctively, Olivia squeezed Anderson's arm.

She willed herself to remain calm.

But she really hoped that nothing happened to

Anderson . . . especially since she was the one who'd talked him into coming here.

Anderson felt himself bristle.

Whoever this guy was, he had a gun.

And he and Olivia were unarmed.

In a condo that didn't belong to them.

Hiding in a closet.

Anderson knew he should have brought his gun. But he'd been afraid of freaking Olivia out. He wouldn't make that mistake again.

He felt Olivia's anxiety. Felt the tension as she gripped his arm.

Anderson braced himself to act—though he wasn't sure if he would muster an explanation or simply fight for his life right out of the gate.

The man paused at the closet and reached for the door.

It started to open when the man's phone rang.

He stepped back and put the device to his ear.

The air temporarily left Anderson's lungs.

That had bought them a little time, at least.

"I'm looking for it," the man muttered into the phone. "Where would she have kept it?"

"I've looked in those places. The desk? No, I

haven't looked there yet."

The man moved from the closet to the desk.

Anderson watched as the man opened the desk drawer. Pulled out a piece of paper.

If Anderson had to guess, it was the same paper he'd just looked at, the one with the strange combination of letters and numbers.

"Okay, man. I found it. I'm going to get out of here now before anyone sees me."

Anderson waited. The man left the room. A few minutes later, he heard the front door open and close.

Anderson's shoulders softened a moment.

The guy was gone.

But that didn't mean that he and Olivia were out of trouble yet.

THE MAN WAS FINALLY GONE.

Olivia waited for Anderson to make the first move.

Several seconds passed before he opened the closet door and stepped out.

Instantly, her lungs loosened.

She glanced at Anderson. "Whatever was on that paper, it must be important. I'm glad we took a picture of it."

His gaze clouded. "Me too. Now we just have to figure out what those letters and numbers mean."

She glanced up at him, earnestly wanting his opinion. "And who was that guy? Do you think it was Abraham?"

"I have no clue. At least, we could kind of make

out some of his features. We can keep our eyes open for him here on the island, just in case."

Olivia glanced around Megan's room one more time. "I don't know what's going on here, but I don't like it. And I think the house on Dagger Point is somehow tied in with it all."

Anderson rubbed his jaw. "I agree. We need to figure out why that is."

Olivia paused. Anderson had said *we*.

Did that mean that he was going to continue helping her?

For some reason, that realization brought her an immense relief.

She'd felt alone and isolated for months now. Having someone willing to come alongside her brought her a surprising burst of comfort.

But now they had to figure out what to do next.

The first step would be getting out of this condo and back to his truck before anyone saw them.

Back in the truck, Anderson turned to Olivia.

He didn't like where all of this was going. Didn't like that Olivia was in the middle of it. Didn't like the warning alarms going off in his mind.

The two of them needed to take a step back for a moment.

"I say we grab a bite to eat for lunch, and we talk this through," Anderson suggested. "Plus, being out and about will give us the chance to observe the people in town."

Her eyes lit as if she liked that plan. "It sounds like a good idea. Do you have somewhere in mind?"

"As a matter of fact, I do."

A few moments later he pulled up to a small restaurant/grill located on the Kiawah River. He'd read about this place before he came here, and he knew he wanted to try the food here. The interior was nothing fancy, but their seafood was supposed to be out of this world.

They stepped inside, thankful to get there after the lunch rush. They were seated immediately at a table near the window overlooking the river.

Before he could even study the menu, Anderson glanced out the window and saw a man standing near the river, looking at the restaurant.

Looking at them?

He couldn't be sure.

Anderson kept an eye on him, just wanting to be certain.

"What's wrong?" Olivia seemed to bristle as she followed his gaze.

"I'm just trying to keep my eyes open." He didn't want to alarm her prematurely. "But, as of right now, there's nothing to be concerned about."

The man turned and continued down the river. Maybe he hadn't been watching them after all.

But if that was the case, why did the tension remain between Anderson's shoulder blades?

The waitress brought them menus, and they ordered—Olivia, shrimp and grits; Anderson, a tuna po boy. Around them, people murmured conversations about the bridge being shut down, about two bodies being found here.

He glanced across the table at Olivia as she pulled out her phone. "I'm not trying to be obsessed, but I want to look up Megan's social media pages. I just want to see if either of the guys are on the island."

"Either of the guys?"

"I saw a picture of her with someone. She had it framed and on the buffet. I'm trying to figure out who this Abraham guy is and if he could be either of the men we saw today."

As she searched, Anderson's thoughts went back to that photographer he had seen taking pictures of them yesterday.

What was that man going to do with those photos? Was he with a magazine? Or had he been hired by a private eye?

There were too many unanswered questions for his liking.

Finally, Olivia pulled her gaze away from the phone and shook her head. "I can't find anything useful."

"Keep searching. If we turn over enough stones, eventually we'll find something."

At least, that was how it had worked in the past for him.

Olivia fought frustration.

It was almost like the questions in front of her were too wide open. She needed to narrow them down, yet she didn't know how. Solving problems was what she did for a living—emotional problems. She should be able to apply some of those methods to this also, though.

Their food was delivered, and they said a prayer together before digging in.

Her shrimp and grits tasted scrumptious with the creamy grits, the spicy shrimp and sauce, and some green onions and crunchy peppers.

"This was a good choice." She glanced up at Anderson and nodded approvingly.

"I read some reviews before I came."

"Smart man."

As she ate, she went to Dana Colorado's social pages as well and studied the woman's picture.

Was she the woman at the house that the neighbor had seen? If so, what had she and Olivia's father been arguing about?

Of all the women her father had affairs with, her personality seemed the feistiest.

Olivia's thoughts raced.

As the waitress came back to refill their waters, she held up her phone and showed her the picture. "Have you by chance ever seen this woman?"

The waitress studied the picture a moment before shaking her head. "No, I'm sorry. But she doesn't look familiar."

Olivia bit back her frown. "Just checking. Thank you."

But the waitress' gaze stayed on hers, and she studied her long enough that Olivia squirmed. Why was this woman looking at her like that?

"But it's funny that you ask me," the waitress said. "Because someone came in here last week . . . asking about someone who looked a lot like you."

TWENTY-FOUR

ALARM WASHED THROUGH OLIVIA. "Asking about me?"

The waitress nodded. "At least, it was someone who looked like you. She showed me a picture."

That made no sense. Olivia hadn't had any plans to come here last week at this time. So, why would someone be here asking about her?

"Do you remember what this person looked like?" Anderson asked.

The waitress stared out the window a moment before sighing. "I'm trying to remember. I'm pretty sure she was a blonde. She was thin. Probably in her late fifties if I had to guess."

"Was she by herself?" Anderson asked.

"Good question." The waitress tapped her lips in

thought. "Yes, she was. She sat just two tables over and ordered a salad with grilled shrimp. She took her time eating. She seemed pleasant."

"Have you seen her since then?"

The waitress shook her head. "No, sorry. And I never saw her before that either. I just assumed she was a tourist."

Olivia stored that information away. "Thank you for your help."

"It's no problem. Enjoy your food." The waitress flashed a smile.

But as soon as she walked away, Olivia turned back to Anderson. "This just keeps getting stranger and stranger."

"I agree. Why would a woman be asking about you last week?"

"I have no idea. At that point, I don't think I'd even mentioned to anyone that I might come here. *Maybe* to my best friend. *Maybe* that I was coming here *sometime*." Olivia shook her head then rubbed her temples. "None of this makes sense."

"We'll keep looking. We'll find answers soon."

But as Anderson said the words, his gaze drifted out the window again, and he bristled.

"Anderson?"

He nodded toward the river. "The man's back."

"What man?" Was he talking about the guy who'd had the camera?

"He was standing out there when we arrived. Looking at the restaurant. I wondered if he was watching us or just staring at the building itself."

Olivia followed his gaze and saw a man in black. From here, she didn't recognize him. But he *did* appear to be looking right at them.

"It's time to stop beating around the bush." Anderson rose, his muscles tense. "I'm going to go see if I can talk to the guy face-to-face and get some answers."

***

"Stay here," Anderson muttered.

Olivia started to say something, but he didn't stick around to listen. Instead, he tore out of the restaurant and headed down the back deck toward the river.

He paused when he reached the gravel and stared at the spot near the river where the man had been.

But he was gone.

He couldn't have gotten but so far.

Anderson scanned everything around him, looking for a sign of the man.

But he seemed to have disappeared.

Again.

He didn't like this.

How had this guy slipped away so quickly?

CHAPTER
TWENTY-FIVE

OLIVIA QUICKLY PAID for their meal before rushing outside.

Adrenaline pumped through her as she rounded the corner.

As she did, a hand flew across her mouth. Another hand clutched her arm and pulled her back, just out of sight.

She froze.

It was the man, wasn't it?

The one Anderson had seen?

He'd grabbed her.

"Stay away," he demanded, his hot breath hitting her cheek. "Do you understand me?"

Olivia remained frozen, unable to speak or move.

"I said, do you understand me?"

Finally, she forced herself to nod.

"Good. Because if you don't, you'll regret it. Mark my words."

He shoved her into the wall before darting away.

Olivia followed his figure as he jumped in a car. But all she could tell was that he wore all black and he drove a white sedan. She noted the license number as the car drove away.

"Olivia?" Anderson appeared in front of her, a knot between his eyes. "What happened?"

"I came to find you. That man . . . he caught me. Told me to stay away or I'd regret it."

"What?" His voice rose. "Are you okay?"

"I'm fine . . . I'm just shaken."

"Where did he go?"

"He just drove away. I should have gone after him, but . . ."

He grasped her arms. "It's okay. It's not your fault. I'm just sorry that I let him get to you. I couldn't figure out where he went . . ."

She had the strange urge to give him a hug, but she didn't.

His eyes remained narrow and stormy. "I think we should pay a visit to the sheriff's office again. I have more questions for them."

"I already paid inside, so let's go."

As they drove to the station, Olivia kept her eyes open for any suspicious vehicles.

But she saw nothing.

A few minutes later, they pulled up to the building housing the sheriff's office, a place that was becoming all too familiar. Deputy Beamer ushered them into his office, where they found seats.

"What's going on?" he asked from behind his desk.

Anderson told him about the man watching them and then racing away. Beamer wrote down the license plate number and said he'd look into it.

"What about those bloody footprints?" Anderson shifted, hoping for more information. "Any updates on those?"

"We discovered the substance wasn't actually blood. It was from some berries that were growing in the brush near the house. Whoever left them must have tromped through that area before walking to the sliding doors."

Olivia crossed her arms and narrowed her gaze with thought. "So, did someone leave those footprints there in hopes of shaking us up?"

"That's my best guess." Beamer nodded slowly—almost maddingly so. "I assure you we're still looking into everything. But we have no answers yet. Our hands are a bit tied with the island being shut off."

"Thank you for your help." But Olivia hardly meant the words.

If Beamer had discovered anything, he wasn't sharing. But her best guess was that he was just as clueless as they were.

That might be okay for him.

But Olivia could feel the danger pressing in. She was the one with the most at stake now and, by default, so was Anderson.

Once she and Anderson realized they weren't going to get any more information from Beamer, they headed outside.

But she wasn't ready to go back to the house yet.

She had too many questions.

And going back to the house now wouldn't offer her any answers.

"What do you say you and I do some shopping?"

Olivia glanced up at Anderson as if startled as they headed to his truck. "Shopping?"

"Not really shopping." He shrugged. "But we could explore the island a bit. It would give us a chance to be out in public. I thought it might be a good move. Maybe draw someone out of hiding in the shadows."

A grin stretched across her face. "It's like you're reading my mind."

"There is a public parking lot a little farther down. We can leave the truck there and then go the rest of the way on foot. How does that sound?"

"Let's go."

They did just that and, a few minutes later, they were strolling through some shops in Kiawah River.

Under different circumstances, Anderson might actually enjoy being here. If it wasn't for everything that had happened in his past, and everything that had happened since he'd been here, this would be a perfect escape.

Another part of him was thankful to be preoccupied with something other than his own problems. Trying to figure out what was going on at the house gave him something to focus on.

As did being with Olivia.

That realization surprised him. He hadn't expected when he came here to meet someone like her. But he was fascinated by the woman, and he wanted to know more. He wanted to know about her past. What her life was like outside this scandal surrounding her father.

But he knew he needed to proceed with caution—for both their sakes.

They got ice cream—Olivia chocolate mint and

Anderson plain chocolate—and then they strolled beside each other. The cool treat was refreshing on the hot, humid day.

As they walked, Anderson decided to see if Olivia might open up.

"So, what's your favorite vacation spot?" he started.

Olivia glanced up at him as if surprised by the question. "That's a hard one. But I've always loved the beach. My father and I had that in common, actually. But we never came here on our family vacations. We usually headed down to Florida. How about you?"

"I like the beach and the mountains equally. But the beach always tends to relax me."

She glanced up at him. "You said you're a firefighter?"

"That's right. It's what I wanted to be since I was a little boy, and that desire never went away."

"Is it everything that you thought it would be?"

He didn't have to think about his answer for long. "I really do love it. I like feeling like I'm helping people and making a difference."

"That's why I like my job too. I can see tangible results." Their steps slowed.

"You're a family therapist?"

She nodded. "I'm like you. I always knew that's

what I wanted to do. In one way, I suppose I was following my father's footsteps. I just never thought that would seem like an insult."

He heard the pain in her voice and turned toward her. "You have to realize that you're more than the sum of your family's mistakes."

She nodded slowly. "Thank you. I suppose I do know that. But it's easy to forget."

"It can be. But remember, condemnation like that isn't from God. The Holy Spirit will convict us. The devil will condemn us."

She glanced up at him and smiled. "I like that. And I think you're right. It's just going to take some time for me to come to terms with everything."

"Makes sense."

Just then, Olivia grabbed his arm. "Look."

Anderson followed in the direction where she was looking.

"It's the woman from the restaurant last night," Olivia said. "The one who was in the photo with Kasey."

His breath caught. Olivia was right. "Let's see if we can talk to her."

They discarded the remainder of their ice cream in a nearby trash can and approached her.

CHAPTER
TWENTY-SIX

OLIVIA KNEW she and Anderson couldn't let this woman get away.

This was their opportunity to find some answers.

But they also needed to be careful not to scare her. That's why they couldn't run after her right now.

Instead, they quickened their steps as they crossed the street toward her. She didn't appear to see them as she stared at a dress in the window of a local boutique.

"Excuse me!" Olivia waved her hand, trying to look approachable.

As the woman looked up at her, Olivia expected to see a flash of recognition.

But there was nothing.

"Can I help you?" She eyed them almost suspiciously.

"I'm hoping you might be able to." Olivia paused in front of her. "I'm trying to find out information about Kasey Winthrop."

The woman instantly paled and glanced around. "I don't know Kasey."

"We saw your picture together on social media," Anderson said.

"Look, I don't know who you are." She lowered her voice, and her words came out more quickly. "But I had nothing to do with this."

"We just happen to be staying in the house where she was found dead," Olivia said. "We're not here to hurt you. We're just trying to find answers. Because whatever happened . . . trouble seems to still be plaguing that house, and we're afraid we might be next."

Saying the words out loud made a shiver wiggle up her spine.

The woman's gaze shifted around them before she rushed, "Someone might see us talking here."

"Name the time and the place, and we'll talk to you wherever you want," Anderson said. "Please. It's important."

The woman's gaze continued to flitter around them as if she were putting herself at risk by even talking to them.

Finally, she said, "Meet me at the Marsh Island Park tower. I'll be there in an hour."

Olivia nodded, her heart pounding.

Maybe this was it.

She could only hope, at least.

Anderson didn't want to get his hopes up. This seemed like an excellent lead, but so much could still happen.

And he and Olivia didn't even know this woman's name. He'd almost asked, but he hadn't wanted to distract her from the conversation since she already seemed jumpy.

As soon as they'd finished talking, the woman hurried away.

She was obviously spooked. But why? What exactly was going on?

He and Olivia continued to try to blend in and watch everyone around them until it was time to meet.

As the sun warmed them and marsh grass swayed nearby, they made their way down the walking trail.

"Are you nervous?" Anderson asked Olivia.

She nodded, her gaze pensive. "I am. I want to

know what she has to say, but maybe I don't. What if it *does* have something to do with my dad?"

"It's like we talked about earlier. You're more than your father's mistakes. Never forget that, okay?"

Olivia glanced up at him, something close to gratitude in her gaze. "I won't. Thank you."

They climbed the tower, but the overlook was empty. All they saw was the marsh grasses leading to the river, several egrets, and some small, skeletal trees that looked as if the salt water had done them in.

They *were* a few minutes early, so maybe the woman was simply running late.

Anderson hoped that was the case.

But there was a possibility something had happened to keep her away.

He knew by the look on Olivia's face that she thought the same thing.

So, they did the only thing they could—they leaned against the railing and waited.

CHAPTER
TWENTY-SEVEN

OLIVIA TRIED NOT to feel anxious. She told herself all the right things to get her anxiety under control.

But it didn't work.

What if this woman didn't show up? Maybe she and Anderson should have pressed her for information when they found her on the street. Maybe that had been their only opportunity to get answers, and they'd blown it.

But Olivia didn't want to think like that. She wanted to stay positive.

Sweat beaded across her forehead.

The sun beat down on them, and she was beginning to feel exhausted. She hadn't slept well last night anyway, and today had been a whirlwind of activity. This whole trip had been, for that matter.

The only bright spot in it all was Anderson. He'd been a true godsend.

As had the advice he'd given her today.

Again, his words had sounded like something Olivia would tell her clients. But hearing the wisdom come from Anderson was a great reminder of where Olivia needed to keep her focus.

She glanced at her watch again.

The woman was five minutes late.

Discouragement wanted to set in, but she tried to hold it at bay.

Anderson reached for her and squeezed her arm as if sensing her gloomy emotions. "Let's just wait."

Olivia nodded, knowing that patience had never been her strong suit.

Just when she was about to begin pacing, a figure appeared on the other end of the walkway.

It was her.

The woman they were supposed to meet.

She'd come after all.

Now Olivia prayed that they would get some answers.

Anderson felt the tension thrumming inside him.

He prayed this would go well.

The woman still looked antsy as she stopped in front of them. She glanced around as if she feared she'd been followed. Finally, she looked back at them.

"Thanks for meeting us." Olivia's gentle voice seemed to put the woman more at ease.

At least, for a moment, the woman's shoulders softened. Then she scanned the area around them, and she stiffened again.

"I don't have much time." The woman's words came out fast. "How did you know Kasey?"

"We didn't," Olivia said. "We found her body beneath my house. Are you a friend?"

The woman nodded, her gaze still shifty. "The two of us went to high school together."

"Can you tell us what she was doing here on this island?" Anderson turned away from the sinking sun.

"I'm not sure. Kasey was working in Charleston. Then she said she had a great opportunity here on the island, so she moved but promised to stay in touch. When a month passed and I hadn't heard from her, I came here to find her. She wasn't answering my calls."

"I take it that wasn't like her?" Olivia clarified.

"No, it wasn't. That's why I got concerned. I arrived here on the island the morning before her body was discovered. I asked around on the island about her, but no one seemed to have seen her. It was weird, like she had never even been here. But then I found out she died." Her voice lurched to a halt as she seemed to fight a sob.

Olivia touched the woman's arm, compassion in her gaze. "I'm so sorry for your loss. Do you have any idea what may have happened to her?"

She fanned her face as moisture filled her eyes. "I didn't even know where she was staying. I don't know anything about her time here."

Anderson knew there was more to this story. "If you don't mind me asking, why do you seem so frightened?"

"Because she's dead! Isn't that bad enough?" Her voice rose in frustration.

"I understand," Anderson said. "But had she'd gotten any threats or something?"

The woman squeezed the skin between her eyes. "I didn't want to mention it, but I'm staying at an inn in town. When I came back into my room last night, a note had been left there. It said, 'Stop asking questions if you know what's best for you.' Now I'm stuck here on this island with someone who may have killed one of my best friends. So, yes, I guess you could say I'm a little bit shaken up." Her words held a biting edge of sarcasm.

"I'm so sorry," Olivia murmured. "You have no idea who went in your room? Did you ask anyone?"

"No, I need to mind my own business. At least, until I'm not trapped here anymore. That's why meeting with the two of you feels so risky." The woman shivered. "That's why I don't want to stay too long. I've had this eerie feeling that someone's watching me, and I don't like it. But I also don't like the fact that something happened to my friend."

"I understand." Olivia touched the woman's arm again. "And if there's anything we can do . . ."

She locked gazes with Olivia then Anderson. "Just leave me alone. Before you get me killed."

TWENTY-EIGHT

OLIVIA WATCHED as the unnamed woman left. Olivia had a feeling the woman wouldn't share much more information anyway.

Anderson leaned closer as his gaze followed hers. "She's terrified."

"I agree. She is. And rightfully so." Olivia turned toward Anderson, her thoughts still churning. "Do you think that Kasey was staying on this island the whole time? Could she have been staying at my father's place?"

"I would think we would have seen some of her effects or that one of the neighbors would have seen her," Anderson said. "I mean somehow, she'd have to get groceries and she'd probably even turn on the AC while she was there, right?"

Olivia shrugged. "I suppose if I could find the

electric bill, I could see if there's been a spike in energy usage over the past few months. That might indicate whether or not somebody was staying there. But, as you know, so far there's been no indication anyone's been there in a long time."

Anderson frowned. "I didn't see any evidence anyone was staying there either. But if Kasey wasn't staying at your father's house, then where was she staying?"

"That's what we need to figure out." Olivia glanced around, trying to gather her thoughts. That's when an idea hit her. "We need to go back to Megan's place."

"Don't you remember what happened last time we were there?" Anderson reminded her, caution in his gaze.

"I do. You don't have to go with me if you're not comfortable. But I might need to borrow your truck . . ."

He studied her face. "Why do you even want to go back there?"

"Because we only made it into one of the bedrooms. What if Kasey was staying in the other one?"

As Anderson headed down the road toward Megan's, he knew this was a bad idea. But he also knew that Olivia was determined to get some answers. He had no obligation to go along. It wasn't why he'd come to the island.

But now he felt as if he'd been pulled into this mystery, and he wanted answers almost as much as Olivia did. Plus, it was good to have something to occupy himself with. Olivia's company had been enjoyable.

In fact, she'd surprised him. Although she was successful and from an influential family, she didn't carry herself with any of the trademarks of entitlement. He also sensed a brokenness about her—a brokenness he could understand. A brokenness that came from living life and being betrayed and hurt and learning lessons the hard way.

They paused outside Megan's apartment and, just as before, he glanced at her. "Are you sure this is what you want to do?"

Olivia nodded, a touch of anxiety in her eyes. That had to be normal. Anyone in her shoes would have to feel some nerves.

"I'm sure," she said. "I just can't let this go. I need answers."

"Then let's do this."

She punched in the code, and they slipped inside

without being seen—at least, as far as Anderson could tell. He'd been on the lookout for any prying eyes—specifically the man he'd seen watching them at the restaurant today.

Something was definitely going on here.

Once inside, everything looked the same. There were no signs anyone had been here since they left.

Wasting no time, they headed straight toward the second bedroom—the one they hadn't had a chance to check when they'd been here last.

Anderson remembered that man he'd seen inside the condo. Remembered the mention of Abraham.

He hoped they didn't run into any trouble this time.

He peered over the top of Olivia's head and scanned the room.

A fuchsia-and-teal bedspread covered the mattress along with some matching pillows. Macramé adorned the walls and the shelves, along with plants. Clothes littered the end of the bed, some toppled onto the floor.

Someone had *definitely* been staying here.

The question: was it Kasey?

Olivia moved toward the dresser and opened the drawers.

Women's clothes stared back at them.

She went to the closet.

More women's clothes.

As far as they could see right now, there was no way to specifically say these clothes belonged to Kasey.

"There's got to be something here." Olivia paused in the center of the room for only a moment before heading toward the nightstand. She lowered herself on the edge of the bed and opened the drawer there.

Papers, pencils, a flashlight, and various books were strewn in the space.

Olivia grabbed a notebook and opened it to the first page. A grocery list was scribbled there, along with various other names and numbers. But nothing seemed helpful.

She kept scrounging through the drawer until she stopped at one thing.

A ticket to a concert in Charleston.

The name on it read Kasey Winthrop.

Olivia glanced over at Anderson. "We did it. We found a connection between Megan and Kasey."

"Good job, Olivia. You were right in following your gut tonight."

Olivia slipped the notebook into her purse just in case there was any other helpful information inside.

CHAPTER
TWENTY-NINE

OLIVIA'S THOUGHTS continued to race as she and Anderson stood in Kasey's bedroom.

Something just wasn't making sense with her.

"When Megan showed up at the house the same day you and I arrived . . . we told her about the dead body in the shower, but she didn't show any recognition, any hint that she had any clue she might know the victim."

Anderson shrugged. "You're right. Maybe she didn't know that Kasey was dead."

"But this definitely connects them. This is where Kasey was staying. I have a feeling she and Megan were involved with some type of illegal activity."

Olivia shook her head as she tried to put the pieces together. Right now, all she had to go on were theories. There was no concrete evidence of whatever it was that could have been happening in the Dagger Point house.

There had to be a way to find out somehow.

Anderson balled his hands into fists. "We just have to figure out what kind of illegal activity that might be."

"Yes, we do. That could be even more challenging than what we've done so far."

"We should talk about this more later," Anderson said. "For now, we should get out of here before somebody else comes back or sees us."

After taking a picture, Olivia placed the ticket back in the drawer and closed it.

She turned back to Anderson. "It is getting dark outside, and it's been a long day."

"It has. I don't know about you, but all of this investigating has worked up another appetite."

"I bought some chicken and salad at the grocery store," Olivia said. "We could cook back at the house. I mean, that is, if you'd like to eat together. I understand if you want some time alone—"

"No, I'd love to."

His acceptance of her invitation brought her an unexpected burst of pleasure.

It would be nice to have something to distract her from everything that had happened since she'd arrived.

A good, normal dinner might do the trick.

"Okay then." She grinned. "Sounds great."

As they drove back to the house, lightning flashed and gentle thunder rumbled. It appeared a storm was heading their way again. Thoughts of the storm triggered memories of arriving here. Of finding her tires slashed the next morning.

She was waiting for the bridge to open back up before she tried to have it towed and fixed. Until then, she was thankful to have Anderson to take her places.

When they arrived back at the house, a package waited on the porch. Anderson swooped it up and looked at the information on the front before nodding.

"Perfect," he murmured. "This is for me. I requested some papers be sent here before I came."

"I guess mail has been able to get to the island," Olivia said.

"This came from someone here on the island. It has to do with my family's roots here. I'll look inside later."

Anderson opened the door for her and ushered her inside. Olivia flipped on the light switch, relieved as soon as Anderson had closed the door again and locked it.

With everything that had happened, Olivia would be lying if she said she wasn't on edge.

"How about you let me get cleaned up a bit, and then I'll head upstairs to help you cook?" Anderson asked.

"That sounds perfect."

As she stepped toward the stairway, someone burst from the kitchen area, shoving her into the wall and then to the floor.

Anderson's breath caught when he realized someone was inside the house with them.

He watched as a figure in black darted toward the back sliding door.

Then Anderson rushed toward Olivia and squatted beside her. "Are you okay?"

Her eyes looked dazed as she peered up at him.

"I'm . . . okay." Her voice trembled. "Go. Go after him."

Anderson stared at her another moment, trying to make sure Olivia truly was okay before rising to his feet.

Then he took off after the man.

Someone had been inside this house, and he

wanted to know who it was and what this person was doing.

He dashed onto the deck, looking to the left then the right.

Which way had the man gone?

Anderson started toward the stairs and scrambled down them. He hurried across the walkover at the dune and onto the beach. As he did, rain began pricking his skin, big fat drops that promised more was to come.

He paused to look up and down the shoreline.

Purple lightning lit the sky.

When it did, he spotted a figure farther down the beach.

That had to be the man.

This guy had made good time. He was fast. Strong.

Anderson sprinted after him.

Before he could make headway, the ground disappeared beneath him.

He landed in the bottom of a hole.

Someone had dug a sand trap.

Now Anderson was in a pit all the way up to his chest.

CHAPTER
THIRTY

OLIVIA PULLED herself to her feet, still shaking.

Who had that man been?

Maybe she shouldn't have told Anderson to go after him. What if something happened to Anderson?

She hadn't been thinking clearly. Adrenaline had propelled the words.

Arms wrapped across her chest, she rushed toward the sliding glass door leading out to the deck. As she did, she pulled out her phone and dialed the sheriff. He promised to send someone out.

She stared outside. What was going on out there?

The sense of urgency to help warred with self-preservation inside her.

She'd wait another few minutes. If Anderson wasn't back, then she would go look for him.

Quickly, Olivia turned and scanned the space around her.

She halfway expected to see that the house had been ransacked.

But it hadn't.

The room looked just as Anderson had left it. At least, it looked the same as when she'd seen the place this morning. The dark blue pillows were in place on the cream-colored couch. The beach photos on the walls were even and neat. The matching rug was lined up beneath a weathered white coffee table.

Next, she checked the doors and windows.

Nothing appeared to be tampered with.

How had he gotten inside? What was that man even doing here? Clearly, he hadn't been waiting for them to return. If that was the case, he would have tried to corner them. To ask them questions or to make a demand.

That meant he was either leaving something here for them to find or he was looking for something himself.

He could have been trying to steal something. But what was there here to steal?

The questions swirled in her head.

Quickly, Olivia turned back to the deck.

She should check on Anderson.

What if he'd been hurt?

A lump formed in her throat at the thought.

Before she could even swallow it, a figure appeared on the other side of the deck.

She drew back, fearing the intruder had returned.

As the man stepped closer, Anderson's face came into view.

The urge to run toward him and throw her arms around him filled her.

But she held herself in check.

It would be too strange. They didn't know each other that well.

Yet another part of Olivia felt like the two of them had known each other for years instead of mere days.

"Are you okay?" she rushed as she opened the door for him.

He brushed some sand from his legs before stepping inside.

A dark and stormy look captured his gaze. "He got away. Someone left a huge hole in the sand, and I didn't see it in the dark. I fell in, and by the time I climbed out, the guy was gone."

Her heart pounded harder. "Oh, Anderson . . . I'm glad that you're okay. I should've never asked you to chase him—"

"I was going to chase him whether you asked me to or not. Someone was in here, and they had no right to be." He glanced around the room as if looking for more trouble.

"Did you get a good look at him?"

"I didn't. He was too far away." He nodded behind her. "What about the house? Is anything missing or disturbed?"

Olivia shook her head. "I looked for any signs of forced entry but didn't see any. I haven't been upstairs yet, but I did call the sheriff's office, and they're on their way."

"I'll go with you to check upstairs—right after I grab my gun." He hurried into his bedroom and emerged a moment later with a handgun. "I didn't want to scare you by admitting I had this. But now I'm glad I do."

"Me too."

Relief washed through Olivia as Anderson took charge.

Somehow when he was around . . . she felt braver. Safer.

Maybe even more at peace.

Anderson stayed in front of Olivia as they climbed the stairs.

If this guy had done something up there, he

wanted to know what.

Although all indications were that everything that had happened revolved around Olivia, he knew that the drama from his own past could have followed him here also. He didn't want to think that was true, but he'd learned to expect the unexpected.

At the top of the stairs, he flipped on the lights and glanced around.

Everything appeared to be in place, from the curtains to the cushions.

Olivia stayed behind him as they crept forward.

He kept waiting for another jump scare. Another surprise.

But he saw nothing out of the ordinary.

That guy had been doing *something* in the house. They just needed to figure out what.

"My bedroom . . ." Olivia said. "He could have been in there."

But when they opened the door, again they didn't notice anything.

Olivia and Anderson glanced at each other, questions dancing in both their gazes.

This didn't make any sense—unless they'd happened to arrive when this guy had just gotten inside.

Otherwise, it appeared nothing had been touched.

Before they had a chance to talk about it, a knock sounded below.

Anderson glanced out the window and saw the red and blue flashing lights.

The sheriff was here.

Again.

He tucked his gun into his waist and pulled his shirt over it, not wanting to add any more confusion to the situation. From what Anderson had observed, his weapon would just be another obstacle to distract the deputies from finding answers.

Would the island's law enforcement ever be able to redeem themselves and prove they were competent enough to figure out what was going on?

Unfortunately, Anderson felt doubtful.

CHAPTER
THIRTY-ONE

OLIVIA AND ANDERSON sat on the deck as Deputy Beamer searched inside the house.

Lightning still filled the sky, and faint thunder rumbled as the storm inched closer.

The weather seemed to match her mood—gloomy yet laced with adrenaline.

As a shadow filled the doorway, she turned.

Beamer stood there. "I didn't see anything suspicious inside. That said, you might want to think about upping your security measures here. See if you can get that camera fixed. Change the locks. Add some new safety devices to the doors. Something is definitely going on here."

"I'll do those things tomorrow," Olivia said. "Providing we can find what we need on the island. I'm assuming there's no update on the bridge?"

"I heard a rumor it could be opening tomorrow. Apparently, the damage wasn't as bad as they thought it was. But officials had to be cautious until they could get the proper inspectors out here."

"That's good news, at least." Olivia tried to smile but couldn't quite manage.

He paused and stared at them both for a moment. "I don't know what's going on here. But I'd suggest the two of you be very careful until we can figure it out. Someone's clearly targeting you. Clinton and I are trying to do what we can to figure out what might be going on. So far, we don't have any answers."

"I appreciate the fact that you're looking," Olivia said.

"Clinton and I will try to patrol past here, just to keep an eye on the place."

They thanked him and then watched as he walked down the steps and around the house.

Anderson and Olivia remained on the deck, looking out at the ocean in the distance.

Olivia froze as her gaze captured something illuminated by the lightning.

"Olivia?"

She continued to stare. It wasn't a figure. At least, she didn't think it was.

Instead, it was more like something being reflected. Like glass.

But there shouldn't be any glass on the dunes.

"I think . . . I think something is over there," she finally murmured.

"Something?"

She waited for more lightning so she could see better.

As purple illuminated the sky, she gasped.

It reflected a camera lens. The man who'd been taking pictures of them at the golf club was out there, wasn't he?

He was nestled in the dune taking photos of them.

Anderson followed Olivia's gaze and saw the photographer.

"You've got to be kidding me . . ." he muttered.

The man seemed to sense he'd been made and rose, about to run.

Before he could, Anderson pulled out his gun. "I have a gun aimed at you. Stay right there. You're officially trespassing on private property right now."

The man stopped in his tracks and raised his

hands, his back toward them. "I didn't mean any harm."

"We need to have a talk. Now."

The guy turned toward them, an outside light highlighting his features. He appeared to be in his mid-twenties, but the fear on his face made him seem even younger.

He didn't argue with them about talking. Instead, he slowly walked toward the deck.

"All the way up here," Anderson demanded.

Hands still raised in the air, the man climbed the steps and stopped in front of him.

Anderson had never seen this guy before.

Not until at the golf club.

So, who was he? That was what he needed to find out.

Anderson still held the gun, even though he had no intention of using it. He simply knew he couldn't let this guy get away again. "Who are you?"

Olivia stood slightly behind him as if fearful the man might also be armed.

"My name is Mike. Mike Spann. I don't want any trouble." His voice trembled.

"Why are you taking pictures of us?" Olivia nodded toward his camera.

"I was hired."

"By whom?" Anderson demanded.

"I can't tell you that."

Anderson stepped closer and growled, "Why not?"

"Because I don't know," Mike rushed, his voice climbing in pitch.

"You need to start explaining." Anderson didn't like wasting so much time beating around the bush.

"Someone emailed and asked me if I'd take pictures of the person staying at this house."

Anderson glanced at Olivia.

"What?" Her voice sounded airy with disbelief. "Who? When?"

"Like I said, I don't know. I only have emails and some electronic money transfers from an unknown number. I was hired a few days ago, and I got onto the island right before the bridge closed. I've been sleeping in my car since I arrived."

"Were you the one watching us at the restaurant today?" Anderson asked.

"Not for long. It was too hot to stay outside." He shook his head. "But I saw that other guy watching you. He looked like trouble, so I went to wait in my car."

"What exactly are you doing with these pictures after you take them?" Olivia asked.

"I'm sending them to my source. As I said, he or she just wants to know what you are doing."

"Are you a PI?" Anderson's muscles remained bristled.

The man shook his head. "No. I was a newspaper photographer, but I got canned because of downsizing. I've been trying to pick up jobs, so I couldn't turn this one down. The money was too good."

Olivia and Anderson exchanged a glance.

Anderson didn't like the sound of this.

"Exactly how much money are you talking about?"

THIRTY-TWO

THE MAN REFUSED to answer Anderson's question.

This didn't make any sense. Who would want to know what they were up to anyway?

"You're going to need to talk to the sheriff." Olivia pulled her phone from her pocket. Beamer couldn't be that far away yet.

"I wasn't doing anything wrong," the man rushed. "I was just trying to make some extra money."

"By invading our privacy?" Olivia stared at him. "That's not okay."

"Look, I don't see what the big deal is." The photographer threw his hands up. "It's not like the two of you were doing anything illegal or anything."

"We want to see your pictures." Anderson held out his hand in expectation.

Olivia's pulse kicked up a notch.

It was a good idea. If this guy had been taking pictures of them, maybe he'd captured an image of the other guy following them.

"Are you sure you have to call the sheriff? Please don't." His voice wavered as he pleaded with them. "I wasn't trying to hurt you."

Anderson glanced at Olivia. "What do you think?"

Olivia stared at the young man a moment. His fear seemed real, and it was true that he hadn't done anything to hurt them.

Mercy or justice?

Mercy—what everyone desired in a bind. Justice—what everyone wanted for those who hurt them.

Love your enemies . . .

The familiar Bible verse popped back into her mind.

Though love didn't always equate with a lack of consequences, she knew what she needed to do right now.

"If you cooperate with us, I won't call the sheriff—for now. Anything changes and I feel threatened by you in any way, then I will. Is that a deal?"

"Sure. I just don't need an arrest record on top of losing my job."

They led him inside. Anderson put his gun back into his waistband, but he remained stiff as if he were ready to act if necessary.

However, Mike was practically all skin and bones. Olivia didn't think he would even be able to harm Anderson.

They led him to the kitchen table and motioned for him to sit.

"I'm going to go grab my computer," Olivia said. "I'm going to want copies of these photographs."

Anderson crossed his arms, still standing. "Good idea. I'll wait here."

Mike glanced at both of them, his gaze heavy and his hands shaking.

Olivia quickly grabbed her laptop before coming down to sit beside him.

The therapist side of her wanted to make this guy feel better. But it was too early for that. She needed to know first if she could trust him.

"Can you send the photos to me from your camera?" Olivia asked.

"I can take out my memory card and transfer them that way. Will that work?"

"Sure."

A few minutes later, images began filling her

screen. While they loaded, she looked back at Mike as he fidgeted. Regret stained his gaze—as well as a good dose of fear.

She leaned toward him and handed his memory card back. "Mike . . . the emails you've been getting from this person who hired you . . . I need copies of them also." She gave him her email address to forward them to.

"Of course. I just need to grab my cell." Cautiously he reached into his pocket and pulled it out. He typed in several things before his phone made a whooshing sound noting that the emails had been sent.

Olivia clicked in her inbox and saw the messages were there.

Anderson and Olivia began reading them.

"Take the pictures. Wherever you can. Whenever you can. No detail is too small."

"For every photo, I pay a hundred. Get some good ones."

"We don't have much time. Sooner is more profitable than later."

"That's all of them." Mike stared at them, hope filling his gaze. "I did everything that you asked. Is there anything else you need from me?"

Olivia glanced at Anderson, wondering if she'd missed something.

Anderson sat beside her and reread some of the messages. Then he shrugged as if he were okay with this. "Looks okay to me."

"Thank you for cooperating," Olivia said. "But I meant my words. If I see you again or if I feel threatened by you in any way, I *will* press charges. Do you understand?"

He nodded quickly. "I understand."

"Now, you should probably leave before the lady changes her mind," Anderson said.

Mike stood so quickly that the chair practically tumbled behind him. He caught it before it hit the floor, and then he hurried out the door and down the stairs.

Now it was time for Olivia and Anderson to study these photos.

<hr>

"There he is." Anderson pointed at one of the photos. "It's the man I saw watching us at the restaurant. Apparently, he was also watching us yesterday when we were at the golf club, but I didn't see him then."

"Do you recognize him?" Olivia stared at the image of the man wearing all black.

Anderson blew the photo up so they could make out more details. "No, I can't say I do. You?"

She shook her head. "He doesn't look familiar. I don't think this was the man who went inside Megan's apartment while we were there. This guy looks taller and broader."

Anderson stared at the man's image. "At least, we have an image now to go on. We could even give this to the sheriff if we need to. I'm sure they're getting tired of talking to us, however."

They viewed the rest of the photos also, but nothing else caught their eye.

At least, this was a start.

Anderson leaned back in his chair and sighed. "What a day."

"I, for one, am starving now. I'm going to start dinner."

"Let me help you."

They rose and made their way upstairs to the kitchen, where Olivia began pulling out the ingredients.

"I'm not sure what to make with this chicken." She held up the package.

He reached for it. "If you'd allow me the pleasure, I'm actually known as a grill master."

She raised an eyebrow. "Is that right?"

He shrugged. "You know, working at the firehouse and all. We do a lot of cooking."

"Then, by all means, you can be in charge of the chicken."

She grinned as she watched him slip outside to look for a grill.

She prayed that danger would stay away . . . for a while, at least.

CHAPTER
THIRTY-THREE

OLIVIA PUT a piece of chicken in her mouth. The smoky sauce mixed with the spicy herbs he'd added.

"This is really good," Olivia muttered.

"I'm glad you like it."

More than anything, she wanted to enjoy this moment. But also knew they had things to talk about.

Things like how to up security measures here.

She swallowed before asking, "Is there a way we can make this place more secure?"

He let out a breath but didn't seem surprised by her question. "I think we—you—should get more cameras for outside the house. I can get some alarms to put over the doors and windows that would alert you any time someone opened one. That would be a great start."

She nodded. "Okay. I'll do that—as soon as I'm able to get off this island."

"I'll do whatever I can to help."

"Thank you." As she swallowed another bite, she remembered that package she'd seen at the front door. "By the way, what was in that envelope that was waiting at the door, if you don't mind me asking?"

"Before all this happened, before you actually even arrived here, I did some research and requested that any historical texts, as well as the original blueprints of this place be sent here. I wanted to dig into my family's history more. A librarian on the island was able to help me, and I'm assuming those are the blueprints since her name was on the return address."

"It's really fascinating that your family used to live here."

"Isn't it?" Anderson stared at her for a moment. "What are you thinking?"

"I'm just running through everything I know so far. Kasey and Megan are both dead. They knew each other, and they both had connections with this house even though their manners of death were entirely different but both found nearby. Someone has been following us. We also know that Megan was meeting with a man named Abraham, even though we don't know who he is yet."

"So far so good."

"Then there's the man who broke into Megan's apartment looking for something," Olivia continued. "We found those numbers with the letters beside them, but I'm not sure what happens when you put them all together. And what happens when you mix all of this together with this house and my dad's scandal?"

"There's no easy answer to that question."

She frowned as she stared in the distance. "I'm just not sure how to fix it."

"Maybe if you get some sleep, that will help you feel better. I hope that I don't sound like I'm over-stepping here because that's not my intention. But I was wondering how you would feel if I slept on your couch upstairs? I would feel better if I was closer, at least until we get these locks changed and the security cameras set up."

Her gaze met his. "I really appreciate how you've stepped up with all this. None of this is your problem and yet you've been so helpful and accommodating to me. Thank you for that."

He squeezed her hand. "It's no problem. I would say it's been fun, but there's nothing fun about murder, right?"

"No, there's not. But there is something satisfying about looking for answers, isn't there?"

"I agree. So, maybe we get a good night's rest, and in the morning things will look clearer. But I have to say—I'm entirely too wound up to sleep right now. What do you say we watch a movie?"

She grinned. "That sounds like a great idea."

Popcorn in hand, Olivia and Anderson sat beside each other on the couch and watched *Castaway*. Outside, thunder rolled, and lightning cracked. Rain pounded the roof at a steady rhythm.

But something about this moment felt oddly normal.

Anderson knew he shouldn't enjoy it too much, especially considering everything that had happened. But how could he not appreciate this moment?

Outside their circumstances, everything about this moment was perfect.

A good movie.

A thunderstorm at the beach.

Buttery popcorn.

And a beautiful, engaging woman beside him.

They sat beside each other, a comfortable distance separating them—a popcorn bowl, for that matter.

The lights were out as illumination from the TV filled the room.

His mind drifted to Selena.

When he watched a movie with Selena, she would always have her phone out recording it all to display on social media.

She'd been what people called an influencer, someone who basically documented her life and got compensated for it. She'd focused mostly on fashion and beauty—two things she was definitely known for.

She'd been good at what she did.

But it ultimately had been her downfall.

He frowned and shoved those thoughts aside. He didn't want to go there now.

It had been three months since she died.

Four months since he broke up with her.

The effects of her death continue to haunt him—and he wasn't just talking about the grief.

There was so much more involved. But Anderson had realized too late that he needed to get out of the relationship.

He stared at the screen.

The popcorn bowl was now empty. Olivia had

pulled a cozy sea-glass-colored blanket around her and tucked her legs beneath her.

Was he imagining things or did she lean closer?

It was probably just wishful thinking.

He turned back to the screen, watching as Tom Hanks talked to a volleyball.

As he watched, he felt something soft on his shoulder.

He looked over and saw Olivia's head rested there.

Then he heard her even breaths.

She was . . . asleep, wasn't she?

He grinned. She'd been through a lot. She probably needed her rest.

And Anderson wasn't complaining.

They couldn't stay here all night. But he'd at least wait until the end of the movie before he woke Olivia so she could get to bed.

In the meantime, he would enjoy the peaceful moment.

CHAPTER
THIRTY-FOUR

OLIVIA THOUGHT SOMEONE NUDGED HER.

She pulled herself from a dream where she'd been trying to navigate her way through a maze-like sequence of events over and over.

None of the tries had ended in success.

As someone nudged her again, she jerked her eyes open.

Credits rolled on the TV screen.

The smell of popcorn filled the air.

Something hard rested beneath her head.

With a start, she sat up.

She'd fallen asleep. Watching the movie. With Anderson.

Her head must have crept down to his shoulder.

Her cheeks heated at the thought.

She glanced at him, suddenly flustered.

"I am *so* sorry." She ran a hand through her hair. "I didn't mean—"

"It's okay." Anderson's voice sounded calm and reassuring. "You needed the rest."

The look in his eyes did something to her heart.

It was more than the kindness there.

There had definitely been a pull of attraction between the two of them ever since they'd met.

Right now, it felt stronger than ever.

As Olivia looked into his warm gaze, everything around her seemed to disappear until it was just her and Anderson.

He reached for her. His hand skimmed her cheek.

She closed her eyes and leaned into his touch.

"Olivia . . . you've been so . . . unexpected. I didn't come here looking for a relationship."

Her eyes remained closed as she savored the genuine sound of his voice.

"Me neither. My fiancé broke up with me when the going got tough, and I haven't wanted to get myself entangled with anyone since then. My father hasn't exactly left a good taste in my mouth as far as men. Because sometimes even the ones you think are upright . . . they aren't."

"I hope to never give you a reason to say that

about me. I've made a lot of mistakes in my life, but I would never cheat on a woman."

"It sounds like God sent you to me this week." Olivia's voice sounded raspy as she said the words. But she meant them. Anderson Scott was an answer to prayer.

His hand moved from her cheek to behind her neck as he pulled her closer.

But he didn't need to.

Olivia leaned into him. Her heart drummed faster as she wondered what it would be like to feel his mouth against hers.

As he pressed his lips into hers, her bones seemed to melt. Her problems seemed to disappear for a moment. The world spun around her in the most beautiful kind of way.

The kiss wasn't long—just enough to be curious and show possibility.

When they pulled away, she stared up at Anderson, wondering what he was thinking.

"We're both tired," he murmured. "And we've been through a lot. But I would love to continue getting to know you, Olivia Beaumont."

"I'd love to keep getting to know you too."

His grin stretched even wider across his face. He took her hand and kissed the top of it. "Then that's what we should do. We'll just have to think of the situation as God throwing the two of us together for a reason. Now, I think we should both get some rest."

Olivia nodded, disappointed to leave him but knowing that it was for the best. "Okay then. In the meantime, I'll grab you some blankets and a pillow. We can regroup tomorrow."

"Sounds like a plan."

The next morning, Anderson was still thinking about that kiss he'd shared with Olivia.

He hadn't planned on kissing her. But there had been something about the soft, vulnerable look in her gaze that made his heart do backflips.

He couldn't remember the last time he felt that way.

Sure, when he'd first met Selena there had been some fireworks.

But with Olivia, their spark felt different.

He awoke early and made some coffee. He wanted to make breakfast—for him and Olivia. Sharing their meals together just felt right.

He paced the kitchen until he found what he needed to make omelets with bacon. And then he started cooking.

As he did, he flipped on the TV in the corner of the kitchen to watch the news.

The first news story caught his eye.

The bridge onto the island was now open. Apparently, the damage hadn't been as bad as officials had thought, just like Deputy Beamer said last night.

Anderson's heart slowed to a thud.

Did that mean he didn't have any good excuses not to look for another place to stay? After all, he was imposing here. Even after the kiss last night, the circumstances of him staying here still weren't ideal.

He didn't want to leave. He'd come here to find out information about his ancestors and this house. Even though he'd gotten the blueprints yesterday, looking at them had suddenly not seemed as interesting. So, he'd put it off, knowing there were more important things to consider right now.

Olivia had forwarded those photos and emails to his computer last night. He hoped to take another look at them today. Maybe they'd missed something that could offer them some answers.

Anderson hoped so.

Because he wasn't sure how many more days like yesterday Olivia would be able to handle.

THIRTY-FIVE

WHEN OLIVIA AWAKENED, she looked at the alarm clock and saw that it was 9:30.

She shot out of bed.

She awoke like clockwork at 5:30 every morning. She had a routine she thrived on.

And she never—ever—slept past eight.

She let out a breath and raked a hand through her hair as yesterday's events flashed back to her.

The danger. The unanswered questions. The unraveling ideas.

Finally, her thoughts stopped on that kiss with Anderson.

That perfect, perfect kiss.

Her heart warmed at the thought of it. She wanted to experience that again. Wanted to get to know Anderson more. Wanted to feel hope.

What would today hold?

As she'd been trying to get to sleep last night, she'd realized she needed to call Dana Colorado today.

It only made sense. Why beat around the bush when she could be direct?

She would do that soon.

As Olivia got dressed, she noted the scent of bacon in the air.

Was Anderson cooking?

The thought was oddly comforting.

She lumbered into the kitchen and paused in the doorway when she saw Anderson leaning over the stovetop.

And, boy, was he a sight to see. He wore a simple white T-shirt that showed his muscles and flat abdomen. His hair was slightly tousled—in the best way. And the start of a beard covered his cheeks and upper lip.

It was a *very* nice look.

He glanced over his shoulder when he heard her, and a grin lit his face. "Good morning. I hope I'm not overstepping, but I thought you might want breakfast."

"That sounds perfect. Thank you."

She sat at the table, and Anderson served her coffee and a plate with an omelet and bacon. Memories filled her. Memories of her dad making pancakes for them on Saturday mornings. Even after she and Rex were out of the house, they'd still met once a month for Saturday morning breakfast.

They'd had such happy times together.

She glanced across the table at Anderson.

Was it possible that she might have happy times again? Happy times that looked different than the past, but that nonetheless could still be filled with joy?

There had been so many moments where she'd been certain her joy was gone forever.

But now something had begun to stir to life inside her.

They chitchatted as they ate, and Anderson told her about the bridge being open.

As soon as her meal was finished, Olivia picked up her phone and frowned.

She knew what she needed to do. The task had been hanging over her all morning.

"What's wrong?" he asked.

"I need to make a phone call and ask some pretty direct questions to one of my father's victims."

"I'm here for you if you need me."

Olivia flashed him a smile, grateful for his support.

Then she dialed Dana Colorado's number.

Anderson waited, unsure how this would play out.

He knew Olivia needed answers and that, out of all the people from her father's past, Dana Colorado seemed like the best option as to who might be responsible for the deaths. The woman didn't seem to have any social media, so they hadn't been able to check her supposed whereabouts over the past week.

Olivia put the phone on speaker and placed it on the table between them.

On the third ring, a woman answered. "Hello?"

Her voice sounded crisp and almost impatient even from the get-go.

"I'm trying to reach Dana." Olivia wiped her palms on her pants as if nervous.

"This is Dana. Who is this?"

Olivia drew in a breath before saying, "Hi, Dana. This is Olivia Beaumont. I'm hoping you might give me a moment of your time."

A brief—yet long—moment of silence passed. "Why would *you* be calling me?"

"I know I'm the last person you want to talk to," Olivia said. "I'm not sure if it makes a difference, but I'm heartbroken over what my father did also."

"Well, you know what they say. The apple doesn't fall far from the tree." Bitterness cracked her voice.

Anderson winced at the words. Olivia didn't seem anything like her father. At least, what he knew about her dad.

He remained quiet, simply a listener during this conversation.

"Dana, I had a couple of questions for you," Olivia continued.

"Why should I answer any of your questions?"

"I'm trying to find some answers."

"And you want my help?" She released a harsh chuckle. "You've got a lot of gall."

"I know how this all sounds. And I'd only call you if I were desperate."

"You have three minutes. What do you want to know?"

Olivia sucked in a quick breath before blurting, "Did you ever come to Kiawah Island with my father?"

Dana hesitated a moment before saying, "Yes, as a matter of fact I did."

"When was the last time you were here with him?"

"It's been a year. That's where he wined and dined me before taking five hundred thousand dollars from me."

That was a good sum of money, Anderson mused. What had Larry Beaumont done with all of it? Had he bought other houses? Where would he have hidden that kind of money?

He knew those were the questions Olivia had to be asking herself as well.

"I'm so sorry for what he did to you," Olivia said. "I'm actually trying to figure out how I can repay some of that stolen money. Do you have any idea what my father did with it? Did you give him cash or put it into a fund?"

"I've told all this to my lawyer, who's looking into this. But since I'm feeling generous today . . . I gave him cash. Not my smartest move. None of what happened was smart."

Olivia nibbled on her lip. Cash? Impossible to trace.

Which was probably what her dad was counting on.

"Your time is almost up," Dana said.

"Just one more question," Olivia said. "Where are you right now?"

"Right now? Why would you ask me that?" Her voice lilted with irritation.

Olivia decided to be blunt. "Someone has been trying to get into the house where I'm staying. I'm assuming it's to look for the money my dad took."

"I'm not in South Carolina, if that's what you're

asking." She let out a sardonic chuckle. "I'm somewhere even better. I'm in St. Thomas."

St. Thomas? She was overseas in the Caribbean?

"How long have you been there?" Olivia blurted, not bothering to hold back now. Desperation for answers propelled her words.

"For the past month. I have numerous people who will vouch for me, just in case you're wondering."

With that, the line went dead.

THIRTY-SIX

"I'M NOT sure if that was helpful or not. There has to be some type of money trail I'm missing here." Olivia frowned as she stared at the phone.

The call had *not* gone as smoothly as she'd hoped.

"We'll keep digging until we find some answers," Anderson said, his voice reassuring.

"I just can't believe my father would have done something like this. You would think after all this time it would have sunk in. But, in my mind, my dad is still the person who took me to the father-daughter dances. Who counseled me on my career. Who cleaned up my skinned knees and gave my boyfriend stern warnings before we went to the prom."

Anderson shifted, his gaze softening. "I know this might sound funny, but in reality, he could be both of those people. On one hand, he was a loving father. But on the other hand, he had a very secret side."

She fought a frown. "But I just can't figure out why. Why weren't we enough? Why did he have to go to other women? Why did he need more money?"

"In my experience, powerful men thrive on adrenaline. Maybe he wanted to test his limits and see how much he could get away with."

Before they could talk about it anymore, a noise sounded from downstairs.

The door had opened, hadn't it?

Then it slammed.

Someone was in the house.

Again.

Someone who wasn't making a secret of it.

Fear rushed through her at the thought—especially since she knew her life was on the line right now.

"Stay here." Anderson grabbed his gun from where he'd left it in a kitchen drawer and tucked it in his waistband.

If someone had come inside the house in the daylight, then they were brazen.

Cautiously, he went down the steps.

When he reached the bottom of the stairs, he spotted the intruder.

A woman in her sixties stood near the door looking at a paper in her hands. A woman who appeared unassuming. Still, caution remained embedded in Anderson's muscles.

"Can I help you?" He kept his tone firm.

The woman flinched, her hand rushing over her heart as her gaze jerked toward him. "Oh, I'm so sorry. I didn't know anyone was here."

"Who are you?"

"I'm Ruby, and I'm here to clean." The woman, whose hair was tucked into a bucket hat, wore red lipstick, khaki pants, and a white T-shirt that looked too big at the shoulders. "It was on the schedule for today at least. Nobody told me that it was occupied."

"You didn't see the cars out front?"

"I figured someone parked here so they could use the beach. People do that all the time around here. You'd be surprised."

Anderson continued to study her. "Who hired you to come clean?"

"Megan. She sets me up to come whenever guests have been here."

"Is everything okay?" Olivia called from the top of the stairs, lines of concern across her forehead.

"Everything appears fine," Anderson told her. "Ruby came to clean the house. Megan hired her."

"Oh . . ." Olivia gasped. "She hasn't heard?"

Ruby's startled gaze swerved back up to meet Anderson's. "Heard what? What's going on?"

Olivia came the rest of the way down the stairs and paused near Ruby. "I'm sorry to be the one to tell you this, but Megan . . . she's dead."

Ruby gasped and stared at Olivia as if trying to ascertain the truth. "What? Why haven't I heard this? God rest her soul. I had no idea."

"It's been the talk of the island," Anderson said, trying to reserve his judgement about this woman and give her the benefit of the doubt. "I'm surprised the management group didn't let you know."

"The management group didn't pay me. Megan did."

All kinds of alarms went off in Anderson's head.

Was this because Megan had this secret operation going on here? Otherwise, why wouldn't she have gone through the management firm?

He crossed his arms. "Do you mind if we ask you a few questions?"

"Sure, not at all. I have two other houses to clean today, but I can spare a few minutes."

CHAPTER
THIRTY-SEVEN

RUBY AND ANDERSON followed Olivia upstairs. She poured coffee for everyone and then sat across the table from Ruby, her thoughts racing.

She had so many questions for the housekeeper, but she needed to be careful in her approach. Ruby already looked nervous as she stared at the liquid inside her cup, and they hadn't even asked her anything yet.

"How often do you come here to clean?" Olivia asked, cupping her hands around her own mug.

Ruby shrugged, gaze still averted. "It depends. It's not consistent, really. I was coming once a month for a while. Then I didn't come for a few months. But in the past couple of months, I've been coming every week or so."

"Every week or so?" Olivia let that sink in a

moment. That didn't match with the other information she'd heard.

"Did you ever meet the people staying here?" Anderson's jaw flexed as if her statement bothered him also.

Ruby shook her head. "No, they were always gone when I arrived. Until today."

Had someone who'd rented the house marked up the photographs? What sense did that make? Who would even do that?

"What about the state of the house after they left?" Olivia asked, her thoughts still racing. "Was it messy? Or pretty neat?"

"Usually, it was pretty neat. The bathrooms, kitchen and floors were mostly what I tended to. But there was one time everything was torn up. It took me an extra three hours to get it straight. It was very frustrating. I have other houses on my docket, you know."

Olivia sat up straighter. "Torn up as in broken? Or just really messy?"

Ruby looked up from her coffee, her gaze suddenly coming alive. "Cushions were off the couch. Pictures were crooked. Cabinet doors were open. But there weren't even any dirty dishes in the sink. It was almost like someone was rummaging around looking for something."

"Did you ask Megan about it?" Olivia anxiously waited for her answer. This could be the clue they were looking for.

Some of the light in Ruby's gaze dimmed. "I made a comment to her in passing. She just said that some guests were like that. She didn't even pay me extra for my time."

Anderson leaned back in his seat. "Did you find it curious that the management company didn't hire you directly?"

Ruby let out a breath. "I didn't ask any questions. I was just happy for a paycheck. It's hard sometimes to make a living around here, especially with the cost of living being so high. In fact, I can't even afford to live on the island. I live closer to Charleston."

"I see." Olivia continued to mull over what she'd just learned. "One more question. These pictures behind me." She pointed to the photos with the blacked-out faces. "Have you seen them before?"

She nodded, something shifting in her gaze. "I have. Last time I was here, the photos were like that. I thought it was odd."

"So, they haven't been like that for long?" Anderson's voice sounded breathless with surprise. "Did you tell Megan about it?"

"No, it must've slipped my mind. Besides, I figured it wasn't my business. The pictures were often in disarray. Sometimes they were all displayed proudly. Other times they'd been put away in drawers. Sometimes they were facedown. Very strange if you ask me. I figured whoever owned this house had some serious issues."

Had some serious issues?

Right now, that seemed like an understatement.

After Ruby left, Anderson and Olivia took a walk on the beach to clear their heads.

Walking—or jogging—had always been a great way for Anderson to sort through his thoughts. The sound of the waves crashing as well as the gentle beach breeze helped.

"Based on what Ruby said, it sounds like my father may have been struggling with what he was doing," Olivia finally said. She strolled beside him, her hands tucked into the pockets of the long, flowing dress she wore.

He didn't say anything, only waited for her to continue.

"I think he put those pictures up to remind him of his family, his roots. Maybe he hid them when he brought other women here. Maybe he really did feel some guilt. Maybe he wanted one foot inside the real world and his other foot inside a fantasy world."

"It sounds like that could be the case," Anderson agreed.

"It actually makes me feel a little better to think that he struggled with his indiscretions. Sometimes I wondered if he even had a conscience."

"What's that analogy people use? It's like boiling a frog. At first, the water feels warm, like a hot tub. Eventually, they're cooked, and they didn't even realize what was happening."

"That's about right. Anyone can lose their way and not realize it. Even me. Even you," her voice cracked.

Anderson could tell she was wrestling with trusting people, maybe even trusting herself.

He paused and turned toward her. "You're right. I'm not perfect. But, even so, I would never do what your father did."

She looked up at him, questions in her gaze. "How do you know that for certain?"

"Because I'm not the type who thinks the grass is always greener on the other side. I know when I have something good." He reached for her hand and squeezed it.

Then he waited for her reaction. Deep down he knew his words were true. He wasn't one to take the good things in life for granted. But would Olivia take his word for it?

After a moment, she stood on her tiptoes and planted a soft kiss on his lips. "I believe you."

Warmth filled him at her words.

Nothing made him happier than hearing that.

As they continued walking, his thoughts raced through everything they'd learned—from the name of the victim beneath the house, to Megan's death, to the items they'd found in her apartment.

And he got hung up on one thing.

One potentially very important thing.

He paused and tugged Olivia to a standstill. "Can I see the photo you took of those letters and numbers in Megan's desk?"

"Sure." She pulled out her phone and searched a moment before finding them and handing him her phone. "Here you go."

He studied the information, his gears turning. "I think I may know what this is."

"What?"

His gaze locked onto hers. "When we went into that restaurant earlier, I saw a sign marking the latitude and longitude of its location."

"You think these numbers are coordinates?" Olivia almost sounded breathless as she asked the question. "You might be onto something. Is there a way we can test your theory?"

"I think so." He typed something into her phone.

A moment later, he let out a breath. "These numbers and letters . . . 32 and -80 . . . it looks like they are degrees that line up with an island just north of here. We'd need the minutes and seconds to pinpoint an exact location. But these do give us a general area." He typed something else into the phone, looked up and met her gaze. "It looks like the island is uninhabited."

Questions raced through Olivia's mind. "Why would Megan have coordinates written down? And what do those other numbers mean? Are they more coordinates?"

"It looks like it. And these extra numbers could be a date. The letters . . . maybe they're a person's initials."

"I think you're onto something." Olivia scanned the list. "If you're right, and these are dates, these other coordinates here correspond to . . . today."

Anderson typed those numbers in also. "Those coordinates are on Kiawah."

"What?" Her voice lilted. "Where on the island?"

"Again, we don't have the exact location, but it's somewhere near the northern tip of the island."

"We've got to go check it out, Anderson." Hope

saturated her tone. "Something's happening on Kiawah today, and maybe it's related to this other uninhabited island as well."

"I agree we need to check it out, but we will need a way to get there. We can't get but so far north on Kiawah in my truck. Based on what I know about this island, the northern end can only be reached by foot or boat. The land is too marshy for any roads."

"How long of a walk would it be?"

"A couple hours, at least."

"I want to go. I want to see what's going on."

He thought about it a moment. He didn't want to put Olivia in harm's way. But he also knew there was no way to stop her at this point.

He took her hand and headed back to the house. "Okay. But we're going to have to be careful."

He prayed he didn't regret this . . . but mostly he prayed that Olivia would be safe.

WALKING THROUGH A MUSHY, stinky marsh wasn't on Olivia's list of top things she wanted to do.

It was taking longer than she'd hoped it would. The sun was already beginning to set, but at least the fading light helped to hide them—too bad it could also conceal any critters hiding here.

Alligators?

She couldn't stop thinking about the possibility. But did they live in marshes? Or lagoons and ponds?

She didn't know, and she didn't know if having an answer would make her feel any better.

Something bit her arm and she smacked at it. Probably a biting fly.

"It's going to be okay." Anderson's voice sounded soothing.

But nothing felt as if it would be okay.

Olivia wasn't even sure what they were walking out to find.

Buried treasure?

She didn't think so. Not with today's date as an indicator. Something about today was important for some reason.

Whatever it was, it might just have cost Megan her life.

Had she stumbled upon something nefarious? Or was she supposed to be a part of whatever was happening today?

Something told Olivia she might be getting in over her head with all this.

Yet she'd come too far to back away from this now.

She continued to trek through the mushy ground, the reeds brushing her skin. The scent of the marsh rose around her, earthy and putrid at the same time.

As she took another step, her leg sank up to her knee.

Anderson offered his hand. She stared it at a moment before slipping her fingers into his.

He pulled her out.

And afterward he didn't let go.

But maybe that was okay. Maybe she should open herself up to more possibilities. Maybe she shouldn't be so afraid to trust. But trusting someone was easier said than done. Especially after discovering what her dad had done.

Either way, she wasn't going to solve anything right now. She'd deal with those thoughts later. Instead, she asked, "How much farther?"

He glanced at his phone. "We should almost be there."

Just as he said the words, a light appeared in the distance.

Anderson pulled her down behind the reeds.

Then they waited to see what was happening.

"Do you have the shipment?" A man's voice drifted toward them.

Although it was too dark to see much, Anderson thought he could see the shadows of two men.

"I haven't been able to get my hands on it," the other guy said.

"Why not?" The first man sounded harsh, almost biting. "You know we're on a schedule."

"There have been some . . . obstacles in my way." The second man didn't back down. "I'm trying everything I can to get to it."

"Trying isn't good enough. If we don't get that

shipment to the right people on time, we're both dead."

"You don't think I know that, man?"

"If you knew that, you would have the goods ready to go. We are running out of time."

The second man mumbled something before saying, "I'll have them for you by tomorrow."

"You sure about that? You already had the wool pulled over your eyes once. The boss isn't happy. He finds out about this and—"

"I know. We'll both die. I'll do whatever it takes to make it happen."

Anderson glanced at Olivia and saw that she was listening intently also.

"You better. Or I'll track you down and kill you myself. I won't go down with you. You understand?"

"Loud and clear," the other man muttered.

Anderson continued to listen, ignoring the marsh grass tickling his face.

Did he recognize that voice?

He wasn't sure.

But he knew for certain that he and Olivia were still in danger—even more so now that they were within sight of these two men.

Just as the men started to walk away, Olivia peeked over the reeds.

As she did, a stick cracked beneath her foot.

Suddenly, everything went silent around them.

ANDERSON PUSHED Olivia down farther into the reeds.

She froze, realizing her mistake too late.

Those men had heard the stick break, hadn't they?

Her lungs tightened.

She'd moved only enough to see if she could make out any of the men's features.

But it was too dark.

Despite that, she was nearly certain one of these men was the one who'd been watching them at the restaurant.

He had the same height and build. Maybe he was the same guy she'd seen outside with Megan. The description fit.

But what did the man want with Olivia and Anderson?

That might not matter if they were caught. She held herself as still as possible as the moments ticked by.

It seemed like everything held its breath. Even the frogs and bugs stopped talking.

What if that one wrong move ended up getting them killed?

Even if Anderson had a gun, this situation was risky.

"Did you hear that?" the gruffer of the two men asked.

"Probably just a racoon."

Olivia felt certain the men were looking their way, searching the marsh for any signs of someone hiding there.

Slowly, the night sounds started up again as if nature decided there was no threat.

"We need to get out of here," the leader finally said. "But tomorrow night. Get it done."

"I will have the goods. You have my word."

The voices faded.

But Olivia and Anderson remained in place for several minutes.

Whatever this shipment was and whatever the goods were, could they somehow be associated with

Olivia's house? Had her dad gone as far as to get entangled with men like these two?

She couldn't rule out the possibility.

And that meant more trouble was coming her way.

Anderson and Olivia didn't speak again until they reached his truck. They pulled off their muddied shoes and tossed them into the truck bed. Then they climbed inside and shut the doors, more silence surrounding them.

They were closer to answers, yet still so far away.

"I need to call the FBI and let them know that something is going down tomorrow night," Olivia announced. "I'm going to call my brother also. He'll know what to do."

"That's a good idea. These guys are dangerous, and they need to be stopped."

Silence stretched between them for a moment.

Finally, Anderson said, "I don't think that conversation we overheard has anything to do with your father."

"How'd you know what I was thinking?" She raked a hand through her hair. "I don't want to believe that either. I just don't know what to think right now."

"Let's not get ahead of ourselves. We need more information before we jump to any conclusions. For now, let's get back and get cleaned up. I don't think those guys are going to come around the house tonight. Of course, we'll need to be on guard, but we can regroup in the morning."

"Do you think this has something to do with the other island?"

"Maybe it's where they plan to meet up with the other guys? It's just too soon to tell. But that would be my guess."

She nodded, almost looking forlorn.

Just as he put his truck into Reverse, her phone buzzed.

She glanced at it and gasped.

"What is it?" Anderson asked.

"I just got a message," she rushed as she stared at the screen in horror. "It's the woman we met with . . . Kasey's friend. It looks like she's being held hostage."

"What?" He leaned closer for a better look. Sure enough, a grainy picture of the woman with tears streaming down her face and a hollow look in her gaze stared back at him. "Is there a message with it?"

"It says: Give us back what's rightfully ours or

she's going to die. Tell the cops, and you're all goners."

Anderson's gaze met Olivia's. "Who would have sent this? What could they be referring to—what's rightfully theirs? And how did they get your phone number?"

"I don't know. The way this is worded, it doesn't match the other texts I've received. But I have given my name and number to some people since I've been in town. Duke at the realty office. This woman. Emma Jean."

"So maybe these guys got the number off this woman they've kidnapped?"

Olivia shrugged, her arms trembling. "Maybe. But for now, I think we need to let the FBI, my brother, and the cops know what's going on. We need to figure out what they're looking for. We need to find her!"

"Slow down a little. Why don't you start by calling your brother? Let's see if he can offer you some advice. Then we'll go from there."

She nodded. "Okay. You're right. We can't panic. But I just don't want anything to happen to her."

Anderson squeezed her hand. "I don't either. We're going to do everything we can to find her. I promise you."

CHAPTER
FORTY

THE NEXT MORNING, Olivia was still preoccupied with the missing woman and how they were going to find her.

She and Anderson had a long—but otherwise uneventful—night after everything that had happened.

Olivia had tried to reach Rex, but he hadn't answered his phone. She'd left a detailed message hoping he'd do some research and get back to her soon.

She'd wrestled with whether or not to tell Beamer. The threatening message had said not to. But sitting around doing nothing didn't seem like a good option either. She had called and told him about men she'd seen near the marsh, and he'd said he made a note of it.

Olivia could hear a mental clock ticking, and she knew it was just a matter of time before something else happened.

How long before the FBI responded? If Rex could get the FBI involved, that would be helpful. Olivia had left a message at the closest FBI field office but had yet to receive a callback.

Finally, after lunch, Olivia's phone rang.

She saw that it was her friend and social media manager, Cynthia Bertram.

Olivia excused herself to talk, wandering into her bedroom. She left the door between the apartment and the rest of the house open so Anderson could relax upstairs where there was more room.

Maybe talking to her friend would help her forget everything that was going on—if just for a moment.

Olivia put the phone to her ear. "Hey, girl."

"Hey, Livy." Cynthia's normally perky voice sounded subdued, almost like something was wrong.

"What's going on?" Olivia's spine instantly tensed as she anticipated more bad news. She lowered herself on the edge of the bed, just in case.

"Look, I don't know what exactly has been happening since you arrived on Kiawah. But I came across something on the internet today that I thought you should know about."

"About my father?"

"No, it's actually about you."

"About me?" Olivia's heart raced for a minute. "Why would there be something online about me?"

"I'll let you see for yourself. I'm going to send you a link to an article. But I wanted to give you a heads-up before I sent it."

"You're making me nervous."

"There's probably nothing to be nervous about. It's all a smear campaign. You know how that goes, right?"

The anxiety inside Olivia surged even more. "Is this more gossip about my dad?"

"Not . . . exactly."

"Have you sent the link yet?" She stared at her screen.

"I'll send it as soon as we end the phone call. But just know, everything is going to be okay. I just thought if you hadn't seen it yet that you should hear it from me instead of someone else." Cynthia paused. "And . . . I've already gotten a few media inquiries about it. I'll hold the vultures off. Don't you worry about that."

"Thank you." Olivia's voice cracked.

Her nerves thrummed as she anticipated what she might be facing.

She'd already had enough emotional turmoil to last a lifetime.

She ended the call and then waited, staring at her inbox in anticipation.

A moment later, a link to an online article posted in a pop culture website came through.

On the front of the article was a picture of Olivia and Anderson having dinner at the golf club. They leaned close to each other as if sharing a secret.

The headline beside the photo read: Is She the Other Woman?

Olivia's heart beat harder.

The other woman? What in the world was this writer talking about?

Anderson wasn't married . . . was he?

Nausea roiled in her stomach as Olivia forced herself to scan the rest of the article.

***

As soon as Anderson saw Olivia step into the living room, he knew something was wrong.

He paused and stared at her as she studied something on her phone with a frown on her face and a dazed look in her eyes.

Had something else happened?

He stepped closer. "Olivia?"

When she glanced up at him, hurt lingered in her gaze. "You didn't tell me."

"Tell you what?"

She held up her phone and showed him a picture of him with Selena. "You were dating a social media influencer?"

The air left his lungs. Olivia wasn't supposed to find out this way.

He'd just needed more time until he told her, until he opened up about that part of his life.

"I didn't see how Selena being an influencer was important," he told her.

Olivia shook her head as if flabbergasted. "She accused you of cheating on her?"

"I didn't. I wouldn't ever do that."

"Mike, the photographer, took a picture of us together and posted on this online celebrity gossip website. They called me the other woman." Pain streaked through her gaze.

"I didn't know this was going to happen," he tried to explain. "I thought I left the media frenzy behind when I came here."

But Olivia didn't even seem to hear him. "I assumed one of my father's victims had hired Mike, but that wasn't the case, was it? This guy has been following *you*. This article makes references to the fact that *I* may have been the woman you were seeing while you and Selena were dating."

Anderson's eyebrows shoved together. "I . . . don't know what to say. I never expected—"

"It's all in this article." Olivia held up her phone again. "You should've warned me that this was a possibility. Do you know how long I've been trying to clear my name after what my father did? And now this?"

He extended his hand, reaching for her phone. "Can I read it? Then I'll explain everything. Please."

Olivia shook her head, almost looking lost for a moment—as would be expected considering everything she'd been through.

It sounded like this article painted Olivia in the same light as her father *and* made it seem like Anderson was also a cheater.

"Please, Olivia. They will do anything to make the headlines."

She gave Anderson a hard stare for a moment before handing him the phone.

Anderson braced himself. He had no idea what to expect next.

FORTY-ONE

OLIVIA'S HEAD continued to pound.

Had she just fallen into the same cycle as her father?

No. She wasn't a cheater. She didn't swindle people out of money.

She hadn't even known Anderson had been dating a social media influencer. Maybe that was her mistake. She'd wanted to trust Anderson so much she'd let down her guard. She'd let herself believe there could be something between them.

Yet she knew from what she'd read that this woman—Selena—had died a few months ago. So, Anderson clearly wasn't cheating with Olivia. Yet the article made indications he'd been a cheater and that's what had ultimately led to his fiancée's death.

Her head still spun.

Olivia had trusted her gut. She'd thought that Anderson was one of the good ones.

To make matters worse, she still wanted to give him the benefit of the doubt.

But what if she was wrong . . . again? In fact, maybe there wasn't such a thing as a decent guy out there. Maybe everyone was just too broken. Or maybe *she* was so broken that she only attracted other broken people to her.

She didn't know.

The last thing she wanted right now was to have a conversation with Anderson. Yet it was like she often told her clients. There was a time to walk away, but there was also a time to listen.

Olivia felt she at least needed to let Anderson talk. To explain his side of things.

He handed her phone back to her, his expression notably more somber. "There's a lot in that article that's not true."

Olivia crossed her arms. "I'll let you start by telling me what in that article is true."

He nodded to the seats at the table. "Can we sit and talk about this? Please?"

She nodded and sank into a kitchen chair.

His chair squealed as he pulled it out and lowered his frame onto it. He stared across the table at her, an earnest look in his gaze.

He cleared his throat before starting. "Selena and I met about a year ago, and we started to date. But four months ago, I broke up with her. I realized something just wasn't right with her, and I knew she wasn't the type of woman I could spend the rest of my life with. But she didn't want to take no for an answer."

Olivia continued to listen, not interrupting.

"Since Selena was an influencer, almost every detail of her life was documented online. Her public image meant everything to her. It didn't bother me at first. Until it did. Then it *really* bothered me. Nothing about our relationship was off limits. She used her posts to try to manipulate me and our relationship. I tried to put some distance between us. But whenever she put something controversial about me online, it brought me back around. I'd find her and demand that she explain or change something she'd posted. But it was all really just a ploy to keep me roped in."

Olivia tried simply to listen, not to form any opinions. "So, she started posting that you were cheating?"

The edges of his lips pulled down in a frown. "I know how it sounds. I know that once someone accuses you of cheating that it's hard to know what the truth is. But I've never cheated, and I never would. In college, one of my girlfriends left me for my best friend. I know how it feels to be betrayed like that, and I'd never do that to someone else."

"I'm sorry to hear that happened."

"Selena just wanted to get me back for hurting her when I broke things off," he continued. "And it worked. Things got heated for me at work. People started to treat me differently, as if they took what she said as the truth without considering what I had to say about it. Then, before I could straighten it all out, she passed away."

"How did she die?" Olivia kept her gaze on him, trying to ascertain if he was lying.

"You're not going to believe me if I tell you." Tension stretched through his muscles.

"I'd rather not believe what this article says. I'd rather hear it from you." She really didn't want to believe Anderson had anything to do with Selena's death.

He let out a long, labored breath. "I was on shift at the firehouse one day when we got called to respond to a house fire. My company rushed there to find it engulfed in flames. We put the fire out, but then . . . I learned that Selena was inside."

Olivia's eyes widened. "Was that her house?"

"No. I think she was doing something for her social media there. The fire started in the kitchen. This is all speculation, but I think maybe she started the fire on purpose. In hopes of getting me to come out there. Of course, I can't confirm that."

"Are you saying she wanted you to watch her die?"

Anderson shook his head. "No, I don't think she thought she would actually be trapped inside. I don't think she realized how quickly the fire would spread. I think she thought if I saw her in danger and rescued her that I'd realize I still had feelings for her. But things didn't work out that way."

"She died in the fire?"

He tried to swallow the lump in his throat. "Not directly. I managed to get her out. She was unconscious and burned pretty badly, but she was still alive when she was transported to the hospital. She held on for four days until her body succumbed to the injuries. I tried to save her . . . but it was too late."

Tears stung Olivia's eyes. "I'm sorry to hear that. I thought her name sounded familiar, and now that you're telling me her story, I think I did hear something about her death on the news."

"Her story got a lot of attention online. A couple of her friends who were also influencers came after me as if I was at fault. As if I hadn't tried hard enough to save her. That if I hadn't broken up with her, she would have been in a better mindset and been able to save herself. They believed everything

Selena had told them. Believed that I had cheated on her and then dumped her."

"And the reporters soaked it all in. Made you into the bad guy." Despite being upset, Olivia understood the unfairness of it all. "And is that why you came here? To get away from all the accusations?"

He nodded slowly. "It's partly why. The pressure was getting to me, and I knew I just needed to get away. I needed to recalculate and figure out if I want to continue being a firefighter. If I want to keep living where I am. Everything that happened really took a bigger toll on me than I expected. I can't help but wonder if I had been a little bit faster. Gotten to her sooner . . ."

"It wasn't your fault." Her gut told her that was true. Anderson would do everything in his power to save someone.

He reached across the table for her hand, but she pulled back.

"I'm sorry, Olivia. I didn't know they'd follow me here. I figured they'd forget about me and latch on to the next big story. I never wanted to rope you into this."

"Now that you've explained, I guess I can understand that. But . . . the article just hit a nerve, you know? I'm going to need some time to think about this. Because now my name is being dragged through the mud again. My career was already in jeopardy. And now this? And you know that there are some people who will read this article and believe it without trying to verify anything."

His tortured gaze met hers. "I know that from experience. And I'm sorry. But I came here to forget about all that. I would have told you eventually. It just didn't seem like the right time."

"Maybe we should just take a few steps back until I can clear my head a little bit more. This is all just too fresh. Too raw."

He stared at her another moment before finally nodding. "I'm . . . really sorry, Olivia."

She was too emotional to come to any conclusions right now. Instead, she stood and pointed toward her room. "I think I'm just going to go lie down for a bit. A nap always makes things better."

But she knew that sleeping was the last thing she would be able to do right now.

***

That had gone better than Anderson had thought. But that still didn't mean it had gone well. Olivia seemed to try to understand his point of view. But he couldn't blame her for needing time.

He was thankful that she was gracious with him.

But the bigger question was, would she ever be comfortable dating someone who might also be in the spotlight? Who might be in a *negative* spotlight?

He didn't know the answer to that question.

He headed downstairs and decided to step outside for a breath of fresh air.

As he did, the house phone rang. He hesitated a moment before putting it to his ear. "Hello?"

"Hi, I'm trying to reach Olivia or Anderson."

"This is Anderson."

"Anderson. This is Duke from the realty company. You and your girlfriend came in here a couple of days ago."

"That's right. What can I do for you?" Anderson didn't bother to correct him and say that Olivia wasn't his girlfriend.

"I told you guys that I would contact you if anything came up. I was going through Megan's office today, and I found a folder that was shoved behind a drawer. I almost didn't see it. But when I pulled it out, I realized it was some accounting for the house where you're staying."

"Is that right?" His heart skipped a beat.

"I believe Olivia was asking about some payments for the property."

"Yes, she's been looking for more information on who's paying the bills at the house."

"From what I can tell looking at this paperwork, there was a trust set up that covers the bills."

"A trust?"

"It was actually set up by a lawyer here on the island. Irwin Gray."

"Does it say who the executor of the trust is?" Anderson asked.

"I can't say one way or another. You'd need to talk to the lawyer."

"Good to know. We'll get in touch with him soon."

"Just so you know, I tried to give Irwin a call before I called you. Apparently, he went to the mainland to do some errands now that the bridge is open. He'll be back this evening."

Anderson thanked him and ended the call.

He needed to tell Olivia.

But first he'd let her rest. They'd most likely be heading out to visit this lawyer as soon as possible. For now, he'd step outside and keep an eye out for either of those two men they'd overheard in the marsh. He didn't know what exactly they were up to, but whatever it was it didn't sound good.

CHAPTER
FORTY-TWO

OLIVIA SAT ON HER BED, unable to sleep.

She had too much on her mind.

She hadn't known Anderson long enough to feel such heartache over this online article. Yet for some reason, disappointment settled in.

How long would she have to live with the media projecting her father's misdeeds onto her? When would the blindsides end?

She wanted to believe Anderson was honorable. In a way she already did. But that didn't stop the doubts from wanting to creep in.

Even if the two of them got along, the circumstances of their lives seemed to be working against them at every turn.

She didn't want to be under the microscope anymore. And if she dated someone like Anderson, that's exactly what would happen. Especially if these bloggers seemed out to get him as revenge for Selena's death.

Could she live with that? She didn't know.

It was like inviting more stress into her life.

Was Anderson worth it?

She wanted to say yes. But, in truth, she hardly knew him.

She had a lot to think about.

In fact, maybe she'd just be better off concentrating on finding the money her father had hidden and returning it to those he'd stolen it from.

Just then, her phone rang. Rex was calling her back.

"I hope I didn't wake you," he started. "You sound groggy."

"No, I'm awake." Olivia pushed herself up in bed. "What's going on? Did you get my message?"

"I did. I've contacted the FBI. They promised to look into her disappearance. I also told them about what those two guys might be involved in, but they've got a backlog so I don't know how fast they will be able to move on that one."

"Thank you. I hope they find her before anything happens to her. That's the most important thing right now."

"I think so too." He paused a moment. "There's

something else I need to talk to you about also. Livy, I saw the article."

Her stomach dropped. "You did?"

"Yeah. Actually, Ginny did." Ginny was his wife. "Who's that guy with you?"

"His name is Anderson. Everything isn't what it seems."

"That's the way it usually works, right?" Skepticism stained his voice.

"I'm working through it."

"I know you are. You're a smart lady. I just worry about you. Is this guy trustworthy?"

She hesitated only a moment. "I . . . I think so. It's been interesting being here."

Her brother's breath caught. "What's been going on? Besides the men you've already told me about?"

At once, she spilled everything to him, leaving out no detail.

"Oh, Livy . . . I don't like the sound of that. You shouldn't have to face that all alone. I should be there."

"I'm not alone. Anderson's here. Besides, I know you don't want anything to do with all this."

"I don't . . . but that doesn't mean I don't have responsibilities. I'm sorry. I feel like I let you down— just like Dad did."

"Don't talk like that," she shushed him. "You're nothing like Dad."

"I think you should leave that place, Livy. Get out of there and let the sheriff's office do their job."

"I'm having trouble letting this go." Even if she wanted to walk away right now, she wasn't sure she could. "Local law enforcement and I don't see things eye to eye. They aren't convinced the women were murdered. I'm convinced they were."

"That's another reason you should leave there."

"I'll keep my eyes wide open, okay? I promise."

He didn't say anything for a moment before he finally conceded. "Okay. But call me if you need me. Okay? Promise?"

"I promise."

She felt lighter when the call ended. Maybe she and her brother would let their father's betrayal bond them together instead of tear them apart.

That would be an answer to her prayers.

She sighed and glanced at her nightstand and saw the notebook she'd taken from Kasey's room. She hadn't had a chance to look through it yet.

She picked it up and skimmed through grocery lists, appointment reminders, and other useless tidbits.

After glancing over the first ten or so pages of

generic comments, she began flipping through the rest of the book.

That's when something fluttered to the floor.

A small paper that must have been stuck between the pages.

Her heart pounded as she reached down to pick it up.

It wasn't a paper.

It was a picture—a candid photo taken on a sunny beach.

Olivia's gaze stopped when she saw the two smiling people there.

It was Megan. Standing close to Olivia's father.

Too close.

While the two of them weren't exactly wrapped in a romantic embrace, they leaned toward each other. They looked . . . familiar.

Acid rose in Olivia's throat.

Had her father been seeing Megan?

Was that their connection?

Plus, Megan had said she'd never met Olivia's father in person. That had been a lie—and the woman hadn't even shown a flash of guilt about it. Clearly, Megan was adept at not telling the truth.

Quickly, she turned it over. There was no time-stamp or location there. But, based on the way her father looked, this had to be taken within the past year or two. In fact, Olivia had bought him that pale yellow golf shirt for Father's Day two years ago.

She pressed her fingers between her eyes as her headache pulsed harder.

As she tried to process that, her phone buzzed.

It was another text.

The end is near. Judgment is coming. Justice will be served.

Anxiety thrummed inside Olivia as she and Anderson sat in his truck outside Irwin Gray's office.

Hopefully he'd be back anytime now. Yet, for all they knew, the man might not even head to the office when he returned to the island. He could go straight home.

But she prayed that something would work in their favor.

After Olivia had received that text, she'd decided to respond. She'd typed:

Please, leave me alone. I am not my father.

There had been no response. But it felt good to write those words, to claim her own space in life.

But she couldn't get those words out of her head.

She hadn't told Anderson. Not yet. Maybe she wouldn't.

There was so much going on already.

After they sat there for twenty minutes, headlights finally turned into the parking lot.

They watched as a man with a balding head and a small build climbed from his car and headed toward the front door.

"Do you think that's him? Is he the lawyer?" Olivia sat forward.

"Let's find out," Anderson said.

Before she could change her mind, he opened the door. Olivia scrambled out the passenger side trying to keep up with him.

"Let me do the talking," Olivia said. "We don't want to spook him."

Someone like Anderson might sound more intimidating than she would.

"Excuse me!" she called. "Mr. Gray?"

The man paused and stared at them, a flicker of anxiety in his gaze. "I'm sorry, but we're closed."

"I know," Olivia said. "But there's an urgent matter that I really must talk to you about."

"Can't it wait until morning?"

"I'm afraid it can't," Olivia said pausing in front of him. "My father was Larry Beaumont."

Realization rolled over his features. "Come inside."

Before he could change his mind, they followed him through the doors and into his office. He set down his briefcase before lowering himself into a leather chair behind his desk.

"So, you're Olivia," he said.

He knew her name. Was that because her father had told him? Or had he been following the news articles?

"I am. I just happened to learn that you and my father were acquaintances."

"In a very professional sense," he added. "Please have a seat." He indicated the chairs across from him.

"I have some questions that I'm hoping you can answer. Important questions." Olivia sat next to Anderson, keeping her gaze on Mr. Gray.

"What can I do for you?"

"I understand that you established a trust that my dad paid his utilities from every month."

He nodded. "That's correct. He paid cash for the

house itself, but the other bills are automatically taken out of this account every month."

"Is there a way that I can access this money?"

He shrugged. "You, your brother, and your mother have a legal right to it. Your father was the executor, but you all were named as the benefactors. However, your father left me with strict instructions that I wasn't supposed to come forth with this information until absolutely necessary. As in, if the money ran out. Until then, he instructed that you had to come to me first."

Olivia paused at his statement. What did that mean? Did her father fear that he might die? Or was he simply planning for the future?

She wasn't really sure.

"How long ago did my father set this up?"

"Fifteen years ago."

Olivia's eyebrows shot up. She'd known that some of these affairs had been going on for at least a decade. But if he'd bought this place fifteen years ago, she could only assume that he'd had some years under his belt before that.

Had he *ever* been faithful to her mother?

Bile turned in her stomach at the thought of it.

How could her father do that? How could he preach about the sanctity of marriage while living a lie?

She would need to call Rex back sometime and tell him about this. She was sure he'd have more harsh words about their father. He hadn't handled things well.

Their father had been his idol.

But, for now, she didn't want to stir the pot any more than necessary. She'd catch Rex up when she had more answers.

She cleared her throat and returned her thoughts to the conversation at hand. "I see. And he instructed you to keep this quiet?"

"That's correct. Discretion was essential."

Of course, it was. "Is there anything else that my father told you that might be helpful right now?"

Mr. Gray shook his head. "We didn't talk about personal things. It was professional."

"How much money is left in this trust?"

"Last time I checked? About five thousand dollars."

She sat back in her seat. "Oh. I expected more. The taxes alone would take up a good portion of that, I would expect."

"There used to be quite a bit more. But, about a year ago, your father took a lot of money out of the account. I didn't ask him what he was using it for. Figured it was none of my business."

Olivia thought through some possibilities. Could

he have been paying off some of the women in exchange for their silence? Had one, or more of them been blackmailing him? She might not ever know the whole truth of the matter.

She glanced at Anderson, who remained quiet but observant. He probably had as many questions as she did about all this.

"What would have happened when the money ran out?" she asked.

"I suppose the power would have been cut. Eventually, if the taxes and insurance weren't paid, the government would put a tax lien on it and eventually . . . well, I don't really know all the steps of foreclosure but . . . that's not on the table now anyway."

"So, what happens next?"

The lawyer shifted in his seat. "Let me know when you would like to access any of the money."

Olivia wondered if there were other questions he could answer—but only if she thought of them first.

She wasn't sure.

But at least she had learned something.

She stood and grabbed her purse. "You've given me a lot to think about. Thank you for your help."

"Of course. I'm sorry for your loss. But you, your brother, and your mother do have one beautiful property. I'm sure Megan probably told you if the two of you spoke before her untimely passing that there have been several people interested in purchasing the property recently."

Olivia paused. "No, she never mentioned that. But we didn't have much of a chance to talk either."

"Well, that was my understanding the last time we spoke. But your father never wanted to sell the place. Said he had too much invested in it."

What exactly did that mean? Olivia stored that information away. She'd have to think more on that later.

"Thank you for your help," she told the lawyer again before leaving his office. She waited until she and Anderson were outside before turning to him. "What did you think of that?"

"I think we have a lot more digging to do."

FORTY-THREE

ANDERSON WISHED there was something he could tell Olivia that would make her feel better. But there wasn't. So, instead, he let her process.

"I found a picture of my dad and Megan," she said as they headed back to the house in Anderson's truck.

He blinked and did a double take. "What?"

She nodded. "It's true. It was tucked in that notebook I took from Kasey's nightstand. I just didn't see it until a little bit earlier today. Do you think . . . ?"

"I'm not sure why they would have a picture together," Anderson said. "I'm not sure why Kasey would have it in her notebook either."

"Good point," Olivia muttered. "That is a little strange, isn't it?"

"I think it is."

"I don't like all the secrets. Why do people have to have secrets anyway?"

"You're a therapist. What would you tell the people that you work with?" Anderson glanced her way.

"'Man is not what he thinks he is. Man is what he hides.' It's a quote from Andre Malraux, a French novelist. I've always thought that was fitting, though."

"If that's true, then what are you hiding, Olivia Beaumont?" He waited for her answer, watching as surprise washed over her features.

Then she shrugged. "Maybe I'm hiding just how weak I really am."

"I don't see any weakness."

She tilted her head. "You don't?"

"I see wood that's been burned by a fire."

"I'm not sure what that means."

"Sometimes, when wood has been burned, it causes its fibers to draw closer together. It ultimately makes it stronger, even when you think it will be the exact opposite. The fires can be like the trials in our lives. What was meant to tear us apart can actually strengthen us."

She flashed a smile. "I like that. Maybe you should be the therapist."

He let out a soft chuckle. "I don't know about that. You're going to pull through this, Olivia."

She reached forward and squeezed his hand. "Thank you."

Anderson shifted, knowing they weren't done with this conversation yet. "What were things like between you and your father before he passed?"

She let out a sigh and shrugged. "I wanted to love him because he was still my dad. And I did still love him. But I couldn't stand by him and act like I supported him."

"Was he repentant at all?"

"He acted as if he was. But I had to wonder if he was repentant for what he'd done or because he was caught."

"It could be a mixture of both."

"Could be. It's hard when giants fall. But my dad . . . he was definitely a giant for me. Or, at least, he was for most of my life."

"I can imagine. It's going to take some time to get over."

"Yes, it is."

Before they could talk anymore, he pulled up to the house on Dagger Point.

As his headlights illuminated the door, he saw an X that had been spraypainted in red across the front of it.

Olivia sucked in a breath, and her hand covered her mouth.

X as in "X marks the spot"? Or was that an X signifying that they were the next target?

Either way, he didn't like that.

Olivia and Anderson sat on the first-level couch, both tired and maybe even overwhelmed.

Neither said much.

At least, Olivia assumed Anderson was as tired as she was. It had been a long day.

"Thanks for helping me through all this. You really don't have to, you know?"

Anderson didn't answer, instead he seemed preoccupied.

As Olivia glanced over, she saw Anderson pick up the envelope beside him. He opened it and pulled out the blueprints to the house.

She watched him as he spread them out and studied them—no doubt trying to clear his head.

She needed to try to get some sleep. She didn't know why she was just sitting here observing him. But she didn't have the energy to make sense of anything right now.

When his eyes narrowed, her curiosity rose.

"Anderson?"

He continued to study the blueprints before glancing around the room.

"What is it?" She moved closer to look for herself, suddenly more energetic.

"Maybe I'm looking at this wrong, but take a look at this space right here."

She glanced at the area where he pointed. But the blueprints didn't really make sense to her. "What am I looking at?"

"I can't be certain, but it almost looks like there used to be a little nook right here that's now closed off."

"Maybe that happened during the remodel."

"Maybe." He set the blueprints on the table and rose, walking to an area that now had wood paneling over it.

He felt between the crevices in the panels, almost as if he expected to find a secret door.

But nothing happened.

Though part of Olivia was curious, she had other more pressing issues on her mind right now than finding a space that could have been boarded up during a remodel.

But she still watched Anderson, part of her wondering why anyone would want to make the space smaller.

After several moments of poking around, he stepped back and stared at the walls again. Then he moved to the stairway and reached for a section of paneling underneath the steps.

He poked around that area, knocking on certain sections of it. Finally, he tugged at the bottom of the paneling.

It started to shift.

Olivia sucked in a breath as she moved closer, now totally curious to see if this was anything.

The paneling lifted as if meant to be accessed. It didn't appear to be broken. It appeared to have been placed there with a hinge so people could get in and out as needed.

Anderson took the light on his phone and shined it into the space.

As he did, his eyes widened.

"What is it?" Olivia asked.

"You're never going to believe this."

ANDERSON REACHED into the cubbyhole and pulled something out.

A gun.

It was one of many stashed inside the space.

These weren't old weapons, not something left here many decades ago when the house was remodeled.

These were new. And powerful. And some were definitely illegal.

"What . . . ?" Olivia stared at the semi-automatic he held.

"Hold onto this a second." He handed it to her before shining the light in the space to see if there was anything besides guns inside.

He pulled a bag out. A black leather duffel bag.

Unzipping it, he saw stacks of money inside.

"Is that my dad's money?" Olivia murmured. "He hid it inside the wall? With guns?"

"It's a good possibility."

She shook her head. "This just doesn't make sense. He had secrets, but he wouldn't have any guns."

"Are you sure about that? This house is being used as a part of a weapon-smuggling organization."

"You think my dad had something to do with it?"

Anderson shook his head. "I have no idea. But suddenly this is making a lot more sense. No doubt somebody would kill to get their hands on all this." He held up the duffel bag. "Maybe they already did."

"I don't like any of this. And I don't even like being inside this house knowing that smuggled goods are in here. What if somebody comes to get this stuff?"

"We need to call the cops. Let them know what's going on. Maybe even call the FBI again."

She grabbed her phone. "I can do that."

But before she had a chance to dial, a shadow filled the room.

Anderson bristled as he looked up and saw a man hulking in the downstairs doorway.

The same man he'd seen standing outside the restaurant.

He glared at them, a gun in one hand and a large black bag in the other.

His square jaw looked tight, and tattoos climbed up his neck. Based on the look in his eyes, this guy wouldn't hesitate to hurt them.

"I'm going to need that bag," he said. "And the guns."

His voice sounded familiar. He had been one of the guys in the marsh, hadn't he?

And he'd come to retrieve the goods stashed here—goods that were worth more than any human life was to this man.

Anderson had to think of a way to get through this situation without anyone getting hurt. "I don't think that's a good idea."

"I didn't ask your opinion." The man tossed the bag toward Anderson. "Now hand them over."

Anderson raised his hands, remaining calm. "Just don't hurt anybody."

"You're Abraham, aren't you?" Olivia's voice sounded thin with fear.

The man sneered at her. "What's it to you?"

"Why were you using this house in particular?" Olivia asked. "Was my father involved with this?"

He squinted as if her words confused him. "Your

father? You think he was the mastermind in this? The only thing he was interested in was those women he wined and dined. His indiscretions were his downfall in more ways than you can imagine."

"What does that even mean?" Olivia's voice lilted.

"That means he finally met his match when he met Megan and started dating her. What he didn't know was that the player was being played. She found out about his double life and used it to her advantage. From what I heard, she extorted half a million from him. Then she got uppity. Her mistake was thinking she could do the same to us."

"Megan was helping you, wasn't she?" Olivia stepped closer, almost as if she'd forgotten the danger at hand. "And so was Kasey. They were both involved in the gun smuggling, but they must have threatened to turn you in or something. You guys killed them, didn't you? You and your cohorts."

Abraham narrowed his eyes even more. "We had no choice. They tried to cut us out of the deal. To strike out on their own. And look what happened to them. We're capable of very bad things, in case you can't tell."

Anderson didn't doubt the man's words. They needed to get this guy what he wanted and send him on his way.

But he knew it wasn't going to be that easy.

"I can reach into the cubby and get what you want," Anderson told him.

"Then do it." Abraham grabbed something from his pocket. Zip ties. "Tie her up first."

"Is that necessary?" Anderson asked.

"I said tie her up! Unless you want me touching her. You choose."

Anderson raised his hands, his words causing a ripple of fear to go through him. "Okay. Okay. Just stay calm."

The guy tossed him the zip ties and instructed Olivia to sit in a ladderback chair. As she did, Anderson took her wrists and bound them together.

"I'm sorry," he muttered close to her ear.

"It's not your fault." But her voice trembled, showing her fear.

"You better do it tight," Abraham muttered. "No shenanigans here."

Anderson made a show of tightening it just for effect and then rose. "Done. Happy now?"

"No, but I will be in a minute." He nodded at the oversized bag on the floor. "Put the weapons and all the cash in there. If you try anything, I'll shoot her."

Once all the guns were in the bag, Anderson added the money and slid the bag across the floor to him.

Abraham glanced back and forth between the two

of them before slinging the bag over his shoulder and taking a step back.

"I wish it was as easy as I said," he muttered. "But things never are, are they? Take another zip tie and bind your wrists together. Use your teeth if you have to."

Anderson wanted to argue, but he didn't. Instead, he slipped a zip tie around his wrists in front of him, formed a loop and then used his mouth to tighten it.

He could still rush the guy. But this man had a gun, and Anderson didn't.

"Okay?" Anderson muttered as he stared at the man in front of him.

"Just one more thing . . ." As Abraham said the words, he stepped back and grabbed a can of gasoline he'd left on the outside deck.

He began pouring it all over the floor, the furniture, and the walls.

The fumes rose quickly, choking the air.

He was going to torch this house, Anderson realized.

And he and Olivia were going to be burned alive.

His throat tightened as he tried to formulate a way out of this situation.

FORTY-FIVE

PANIC RACED through Olivia as the scent of gasoline surrounded her.

No . . .

She glanced at Anderson and saw the concern in his gaze.

This was bad . . . really, really bad.

She began pulling at the ties around her wrists, ties that bound her to the chair.

There was no use.

She'd never get them off in time.

"You don't have to do this!" She didn't bother to hide the desperation in her voice.

"Unfortunately, I do." Abraham smirked as he paused near the door. "I tried to warn you guys to stay away, to get out of the house. But you didn't listen. I had to get access to these guns."

"You left those footprints, didn't you?" Anderson asked.

"Like I said, I tried to warn you."

"What about the texts?" Olivia asked. "Did you send them?"

"What texts?" Abraham practically snorted. "I don't know anything about any texts. But I followed you. I got worried that you might know something. Then I realized you didn't. But you're still in my way, and I need to fix that. Otherwise, it's my head on the platter." He poured the rest of the gasoline and tossed the can away.

Olivia tried to swallow, but her throat felt swollen. The scent of gasoline made her want to gag. But it was mostly fear she felt . . . fear that nearly strangled her.

"Sorry about this. But . . . take care." He pulled out a lighter and tossed it.

Before he could dart out the door, flames filled the place with a loud whoosh, trailing the gasoline he'd left.

"Anderson . . ." Olivia's gaze shot toward him, her voice trembling uncontrollably.

"Just stay calm," he said. "I'm trying to get this zip tie from around my wrists. I'll be free in a second."

She coughed, the smoke already filling her lungs.

The walls burst into flames quickly. So quickly.

As the flames licked closer to her legs, more panic chased her.

How were they going to get out of this?

Using his teeth, Anderson got the zip tie from his wrists.

He rushed to Olivia, desperate to rescue her.

Smoke filled the air as a smoke alarm blared.

They had less than five minutes to get out of this place before the fire got to them.

He coughed before pulling his shirt over his mouth.

"Anderson . . ." Olivia's voice cracked with desperation.

Instead of untying her, he lifted her and the chair together. It was the quickest way to get her out of here.

Coughing again, he ducked low and headed to the sliding glass door.

As flames flared to life in front of him, he paused.

He set Olivia down for long enough to grab a throw blanket from the couch. He doused the flames enough to grab Olivia again and dart across.

Finally, he ran outside. As heat spilled from the

doorway, he set Olivia down and used a knife in his pocket to cut the plastic at her wrists.

Then he grabbed her hand and dragged her away from the house, toward the driveway.

Finally, they could breathe. They took in deep gulps of fresh air.

It looked as if they were safe—for now.

But when he saw Abraham lying unconscious on the ground, he froze.

This wasn't over yet, was it?

CHAPTER
FORTY-SIX

OLIVIA SUCKED in a breath when she saw a redhead standing in front of her.

She looked familiar but different . . .

Then it hit her.

"Ruby?" This was the woman who'd come to clean the house.

But she must have been wearing a wig before. Because now her hair was bright red and pulled into a bun.

The woman scowled at them, a gun in her hands. "Your father ruined my family. Now I'm going to ruin his."

Anderson edged in front of Olivia. "Let's wait a second here. Olivia didn't do anything. Her father is already dead."

"I want your family to suffer, just like my daughter suffered."

"Who are you really?" Olivia asked. "Help me understand."

She scowled again. "I'm Dana's mom. Your father used her. He broke her spirit. She acts like she's doing well, but she's not. She keeps jumping from man to man. She's not right. She'll never be right again."

"I'm sorry to hear that." Olivia flinched as a pop sounded in the house behind her.

Anderson covered her, pushing her away from the growing fire.

But Ruby stopped them from going any farther. She raised her gun and sneered.

"It's time for justice to be served," she muttered.

"Wait. You sent me all those texts?" Olivia stilled. "Those warnings?"

"So, what if I did? I wanted you to feel the fear. To have to look over your shoulder. To wonder what was going to happen next. Somebody has to pay for your father's sins."

"Haven't we all paid enough already?" Olivia asked, trying to get through to her. "Hurting us won't change anything. It won't undo the past."

"We need to get farther away from this house," Anderson said. "It's about to collapse."

As if to confirm his statement, a fiery board landed in the grass beside them.

Sirens wailed in the distance.

Someone must've seen the smoke and called for help.

Firefighters were on their way.

Olivia wanted to be relieved. But couldn't. Not yet.

Would they be too late?

Tension grew between Anderson's shoulders.

They needed to get away from this house. Now.

But Ruby didn't appear to be in the mood to listen.

"Can't we just talk about this like adults?" Anderson said, trying to extinguish the situation.

"I'm tired of talking. Tired of empty promises. Tired of waiting for God to take away this pain."

Olivia stepped closer. "I know it may feel impossible now. But it's not impossible for God to heal this situation—and the hurt you feel. But this isn't the way to do this."

Another pop sounded behind them, and wooden siding crashed to the ground.

Anderson felt the heat of the fire, felt the danger growing closer as part of the deck went up in flames.

"You're great at giving advice, aren't you?" Ruby sneered. "Just like your father. Hypocrites. Both of you."

"I'm imperfect, if that's what you're saying," Olivia said. "But the only one to blame for what he did is my father himself."

Anderson had to admire how calm Olivia was, especially in light of their circumstances.

But they needed to get away from this burning house. They had no time to lose.

More flames roared to life behind him.

"Your father ruined my daughter's life!" Ruby shouted, seemingly oblivious to the fire. "It's time for me to ruin yours."

Just as she said the words, flaming debris tumbled from the house—toward Ruby.

"Get down!" In one motion, Olivia threw herself over Ruby and rolled with her out of the way of the burning pieces of wood just in time.

Anderson rushed toward them, taking the gun from Ruby's hand. "Are you both okay?"

Ruby looked up at Olivia, a stunned look in her eyes, almost as if she didn't know what to say.

Before she could say anything else, the sheriff and fire department arrived on the scene.

First responders took over—arresting Ruby, checking on Abraham, questioning Anderson and Olivia. From what he overheard Ruby saying, the woman had hit Abraham over the head with her gun and knocked him out. He'd begun to regain consciousness as the paramedics examined him.

Anderson knew they had a long night ahead of them—a long night of explaining everything that had just happened.

But most of all, he was simply thankful they had all survived.

OLIVIA STILL COULDN'T BELIEVE how everything had gone down.

The murders.

The gun smuggling.

The mother bent on revenge.

But at least it was all finally over.

The sheriff had wanted Olivia to press charges against Ruby. But she didn't. The woman was simply hurting and needed counseling more than anything. Olivia suspected she was the one who'd scribbled out the faces on those photos, probably sometime when she'd come to clean.

Glenda Campbell—Kasey's friend—had been found tied up in the apartment where Abraham was staying. She was shaken but okay. Thankfully,

Abraham hadn't hurt her—he'd only threatened to do so. Mostly, Glenda had been leverage.

Abraham was arrested, along with the other man from the marsh. They'd been running a weapons operation all up and down the East Coast. They used those coordinates to plan their drops.

Megan had helped the smugglers—until she'd turned the tables. That's when they'd killed her.

Apparently, Megan thought she'd use the money she'd extorted out of Olivia's dad to buy her way to the top of the gun-smuggling business.

Those poofy footstools Olivia had seen in Megan's condo? They were actually filled with cash. Glenda had said that Kasey mentioned Megan had started creating those poofs herself as a new hobby. Everyone who knew Megan agreed that didn't sound like something that fit her personality.

The FBI had checked one and discovered the cash inside.

Olivia was trying to work out a deal right now to use that money to pay back the victims. She was in talks with a lawyer to see how she could liquify any other assets.

Especially since Seacret Hideout was a total loss.

Turns out the house had been built from wreckage of old ships. It had been saved once from a fire. Now it had been burned to the bones again and would need to be rebuilt. Olivia couldn't help but think about how that symbolized her life as well. All the superficial things that had defined her had been stripped away, leaving just a foundation to stand on.

But, just like The House on Dagger Point, she could also rebuild—and she planned on doing just that.

Those million-dollar house listings that Megan had sitting around in her place?

She didn't have those because she wanted to sell the homes. She had them because she wanted to buy one of the houses to use as a base of operations for the gun smuggling. Since the Beaumont family had inherited the house, Megan knew it was only a matter of time before she wouldn't be able to use it anymore.

"You chose mercy," Anderson muttered as they walked along the beach.

His voice pulled Olivia from her heavy thoughts.

The two of them had gotten two separate hotel rooms in Folly Beach. They needed to stay in the area to answer any questions the sheriff had. They'd had to purchase some new clothes and other items— enough to last for a week or so.

But that was okay because neither of them were ready to leave this place yet.

But Olivia dreaded this conversation. She knew

Anderson really had no reason to stay on the island, especially not now that the media had discovered his whereabouts.

She wasn't ready to tell him goodbye yet. She wasn't ready for him to leave, to be out of her life.

She paused and glanced up at him. "If I want mercy myself then I should choose it for others, right?"

"I like the way you think." His smile slipped. "I think we should talk about the future."

She held back a frown. "I suppose that's a good idea."

"I talked to the county fire inspector today," he started. "I hope you don't mind that I took that liberty. But even though the house was a total loss, you should be able to salvage some of the original lumber. I think some of it can be restored."

Her eyebrows shot up. "Really? I love that idea."

He nodded, his hands in his pockets. "I do too. I have a proposal for you."

"A proposal?" Her gaze lit with exaggerated curiosity.

"Not that kind of proposal." He chuckled. "I was actually wondering if I might help you build a new house on Dagger Point using the original wood for some of the ornamental beams. I know I'm probably overstepping—"

"No, you're not. I think that's an awesome idea."

Visible relief washed through him. "Really? That's fantastic. I've never asked you what you planned on doing with the property. So, I wasn't sure—"

"Insurance should pay to rebuild it. At first, I thought about selling the land and using that and the insurance money to repay the victims. But now I'm wondering if I should start some kind of retreat center to help people who've been hurt by people in positions of leadership. As a licensed therapist, I could run the program. I could use the profits to repay the victims."

"I think that sounds like a great idea."

Warmth filled her at his approval. Not that she needed it. But it was still nice.

"How about you? I mean, I know you said you wanted to help rebuild but you have a life waiting for you back in Jacksonville."

He shrugged. "I was thinking about hanging here for a while. In fact, I talked to the fire department in Charleston, and they're hiring. The chief offered me a job."

"You're willing to move to this area?" Warmth spread through her at the thought.

He stepped closer. "I was hoping you might stick around also."

More warmth oozed inside her. "Well, I can think

of a reason or two to move to the island. Especially if I'm going to be running a retreat center. And . . . I don't know. Dating a handsome firefighter?"

A smile stretched across his face. "I was hoping you'd say that. So, I guess that means you've accepted my proposal?"

Olivia grinned, rose to her tiptoes, and answered with a long, heartfelt kiss.

~~~

If you enjoyed this book, please consider leaving a review!

Stay tuned for *The Bungalow on Shadow Road*.

~~~

ALSO BY CHRISTY BARRITT:

OTHER BOOKS IN THE BEACH HOUSE MYSTERY SERIES:

Each house has a history. Each person has a secret. Each turn of events leads to danger.

The Cottage on Ghost Lane

Come back to me.

Cole Dalton's wife, Caroline, had the words etched onto a pendant for him. Each time he deployed overseas as a military bomb tech, she stitched the pendant into his uniform. Cole returned safely from the battlefield . . . only to bury his wife after a tragic car accident.

Cole moves into their beachside cottage to both heal and find closure after Caroline's death. But on the first day he arrives, he finds an intruder searching for something and desperate enough to kill.

Mysterious incidents continue to occur, leading Cole to ask: Was Caroline hiding something in the months before she died? But what? And why?

As danger closes in and a storm lingers off the coast, Cole must find answers. But ghosts of the past have a stranglehold on him. With his heart on the line, he must overcome the grief haunting him . . . or his story will become part of his cottage's tragic history.

The Inn on Hanging Hill

Lindsey Waters never wanted to return to the seaside inn where she grew up. Too many traumatic memories haunt the place, both from her childhood and from days gone by. But with guilt relentlessly chasing her after a tragic choice, she's desperate for a fresh start.

Mysterious incidents begin plaguing the inn —*dangerous* incidents—that make it clear someone wants to scare Lindsey away. But why? Does it have anything to do with the two weeks missing from her memory when she was abducted at age twelve?

Childhood friend Benjamin Newsom seems like an answer to prayer when he shows up to work as a handyman. But something is different about him, something Lindsey can't put her finger on. She's certain Benjamin harbors secrets.

As peril continues to close in, Lindsey must decide if she wants to face her past or run. She doesn't know whom she can trust, and whatever choices she makes will determine if she lives or if she becomes part of the inn's tragic legacy.

YOU ALSO MIGHT ENJOY: FOG LAKE SUSPENSE

Edge of Peril

When evil descends like fog on a mountain community, no one feels safe. After hearing about a string of murders in a Smoky Mountain town, journalist Harper Jennings realizes a startling truth. She knows who may be responsible—the same person who tried to kill her three years ago. Now Harper must convince the cops to believe her before the killer strikes again. Sheriff Luke Wilder returned to his hometown, determined to keep the promise he made to his dying father. The sleepy tourist area with a tragic past hadn't seen a murder in decades—until now. Keeping the community safe seems impossible as darkness edges closer, threatening to consume everything in its path. As The Watcher grows desperate, Harper and Luke must work together in order to defeat him. But the peril around them escalates, making it clear the killer will stop at nothing to get what he wants.

Margin of Error

Some secrets have deadly consequences. Brynlee Parker thought her biggest challenge would be hiking to Dead Man's Bluff and fulfilling her dad's last wishes. She never thought she'd witness two men being viciously murdered while on a mountainous trail. Even worse, the deadly predator is now hunting her. Boone Wilder wants nothing to do with Dead Man's Bluff, not after his wife died there. But he can't seem to mind his own business when a mysterious out-of-towner burst into his camp store in a frenzied panic. Something—or someone—deadly is out there. The killer's hunger for blood seems to be growing at a brutal pace. Can Brynlee and Boone figure out who's behind these murders? Or will the hurts and secrets from their past not allow for even a margin of error?

Brink of Danger

Ansley Wilder has always lived life on the wild side, using thrills to numb the pain from her past and escape her mistakes. But a near-death experience two years ago changed everything. When another incident nearly claims her life, she turns her thrill-seeking ways into a fight for survival. Ryan Philips left Fog Lake to chase adventure far from home. Now he's returned as the new fire chief in town, but the slower paced life he seeks is nowhere to be found. Not only is a wildfire blazing out of control, but a malicious killer known as "The Woodsman" is enacting crimes that appear accidental. Plus, there seems to be a strange connection with these incidents and his best friend's little sister, Ansley Wilder. As a killer watches their every move and the forest fire threatens to destroy their scenic town, both Ryan and Ansley hover on the brink of danger. One wrong move could send them tumbling over the edge . . . permanently.

Line of Duty

Jaxon Wilder didn't plan on returning home to Fog Lake, Tennessee, following his tour of duty in Iraq. But after a gut-wrenching failure during his stint in the Army, he now faces a new challenge: his family. Abby Brennan always did her best to be the good girl and to live by the rules. When a wrong decision changes her entire life, she tries to hide from the world. However, a madman known as the Executioner is determined to find her and enact his own brand of justice. When Jaxon and Abby are thrown together in the killer's crosshairs, they're forced to depend on one another to survive. Will Jaxon's sense of duty be enough to help keep Abby safe? Or will deadly secrets lead to the penalty of death?

Legacy of Lies

The justice system failed her family—and so did her hometown. Madison Colson knows deep down that her father—a convicted serial killer—is innocent. But believing it and proving it are two entirely different things. Unable to help her father, Madison has spent most of her adult life overcompensating by helping others. When her aunt dies unexpectantly, duty calls her back to Fog Lake, Tennessee, a beautiful but painful place she'd rather forget. Terrifying events begin to unfold once she arrives, unleashing her worst nightmares. The Good Samaritan Killer—or a copycat—is back, and now Madison Colson is his target. FBI Special Agent Shane Townsend is determined to stop the deadly rampage that has sent the tightknit community into a frenzy. But he needs to earn Madison's trust first. The task feels impossible, especially considering his father is the one who put her dad in prison. With the whole town on edge and pointing fingers, tension escalates out of control. Madison and Shane must sort the facts from the lies—and fight for a legacy of truth—before The Good Samaritan Killer has the final say.

Secrets of Shame

A killer has a promise to keep . . . Attorney Isaac Colson only wants to put his tumultuous past in Fog Lake behind him and return to his life in Memphis. But when an ominous text threatens that he must come back or there will be deadly consequences, he knows he can't take any chances. Rebecca Moreno has only ever loved one man—her high school sweetheart, Isaac Colson. But when his dad went to prison for murder, Rebecca's father forbade them from seeing each other again. Years later, Isaac is back in town and old feelings are stirring. But Rebecca is harboring a secret that could change everything. When The Good Samaritan Killer strikes again, guilt pummels her. She has to tell Isaac the truth. But as events unfold, she has more to lose than ever. Isaac and Rebecca must find answers—their lives depend on it. But everyone seems to have secrets, each that forms an obstacle to finding the truth . . . and to staying alive.

Refuge of Redemption

Home is a place of refuge—unless it's a killer's playground. For years, Bear Colson has been known as the serial killer's son. But now, someone else is behind bars for the crimes his father was accused of committing. Bear wants to believe hope for a brighter future is in sight, but he has reason to suspect more than one killer was involved. Forensic photographer Piper Stephens' career crashed and burned when she trusted the wrong man. Now, after discovering an alarming secret about the infamous Good Samaritan Killer, she sets out to find both answers and redemption. But things go awry when her assistant becomes the next victim. As fear batters Fog Lake residents once again, Bear and Piper join forces to track down the truth. But the killer is determined to remain in the shadows—and he'll destroy anyone who stands in his way.

ABOUT THE AUTHOR

USA Today has called Christy Barritt's books "scary, funny, passionate, and quirky."

Christy writes both mystery and romantic suspense novels that are clean with underlying messages of faith. Her books have won the Daphne du Maurier Award for Excellence in Suspense and Mystery, have been twice nominated for the Romantic Times Reviewers' Choice Award, and have finaled for both a Carol Award and Foreword Magazine's Book of the Year.

She is married to her Prince Charming, a man who thinks she's hilarious—but only when she's not trying to be. Christy is a self-proclaimed klutz, an avid music lover who's known for spontaneously bursting into song, and a road trip aficionado.

When she's not working or spending time with her family, she enjoys singing, playing the guitar, and exploring small, unsuspecting towns where people have no idea how accident-prone she is.

Find Christy online at:
www.christybarritt.com
www.facebook.com/christybarritt
www.twitter.com/cbarritt

Sign up for Christy's newsletter to get information on all of her latest releases here: **www.christybarritt. com/newsletter-sign-up/**

COMPLETE BOOK LIST

Squeaky Clean Mysteries:
- #1 Hazardous Duty
- #2 Suspicious Minds
- #2.5 It Came Upon a Midnight Crime (novella)
- #3 Organized Grime
- #4 Dirty Deeds
- #5 The Scum of All Fears
- #6 To Love, Honor and Perish
- #7 Mucky Streak
- #8 Foul Play
- #9 Broom & Gloom
- #10 Dust and Obey
- #11 Thrill Squeaker
- #11.5 Swept Away (novella)
- #12 Cunning Attractions
- #13 Cold Case: Clean Getaway

#14 Cold Case: Clean Sweep

#15 Cold Case: Clean Break

#16 Cleans to an End

While You Were Sweeping, A Riley Thomas Spinoff

The Sierra Files:

#1 Pounced

#2 Hunted

#3 Pranced

#4 Rattled

The Gabby St. Claire Diaries (a Tween Mystery series):

The Curtain Call Caper

The Disappearing Dog Dilemma

The Bungled Bike Burglaries

The Worst Detective Ever

#1 Ready to Fumble

#2 Reign of Error

#3 Safety in Blunders

#4 Join the Flub

#5 Blooper Freak

#6 Flaw Abiding Citizen

#7 Gaffe Out Loud

#8 Joke and Dagger

#9 Wreck the Halls

#10 Glitch and Famous

Raven Remington

Relentless

Holly Anna Paladin Mysteries:

#1 Random Acts of Murder

#2 Random Acts of Deceit

#2.5 Random Acts of Scrooge

#3 Random Acts of Malice

#4 Random Acts of Greed

#5 Random Acts of Fraud

#6 Random Acts of Outrage

#7 Random Acts of Iniquity

Lantern Beach Mysteries

#1 Hidden Currents

#2 Flood Watch

#3 Storm Surge

#4 Dangerous Waters

#5 Perilous Riptide

#6 Deadly Undertow

Lantern Beach Romantic Suspense

Tides of Deception

Shadow of Intrigue

Storm of Doubt
Winds of Danger
Rains of Remorse
Torrents of Fear

Lantern Beach P.D.
On the Lookout
Attempt to Locate
First Degree Murder
Dead on Arrival
Plan of Action

Lantern Beach Escape
Afterglow (a novelette)

Lantern Beach Blackout
Dark Water
Safe Harbor
Ripple Effect
Rising Tide

Lantern Beach Guardians
Hide and Seek
Shock and Awe
Safe and Sound

Lantern Beach Blackout: The New Recruits

Rocco

Axel

Beckett

Gabe

Lantern Beach Mayday

Run Aground

Dead Reckoning

Tipping Point

Lantern Beach Blackout: Danger Rising

Brandon

Dylan

Maddox

Titus

Lantern Beach Christmas

Silent Night

Crime á la Mode

Dead Man's Float

Milkshake Up

Bomb Pop Threat

Banana Split Personalities

Vanishing Ranch

Forgotten Secrets

Necessary Risk (coming soon)

The Sidekick's Survival Guide

The Art of Eavesdropping

The Perks of Meddling

The Exercise of Interfering

The Practice of Prying

The Skill of Snooping

The Craft of Being Covert

Saltwater Cowboys

Saltwater Cowboy

Breakwater Protector

Cape Corral Keeper

Seagrass Secrets

Driftwood Danger

Unwavering Security

Beach House Mysteries

The Cottage on Ghost Lane

The Inn on Hanging Hill

The House on Dagger Point

School of Hard Rocks Mysteries

The Treble with Murder

Crime Strikes a Chord

Tone Death (coming soon)

Carolina Moon Series
  Home Before Dark
  Gone By Dark
  Wait Until Dark
  Light the Dark
  Taken By Dark

Suburban Sleuth Mysteries:
  Death of the Couch Potato's Wife

Fog Lake Suspense:
  Edge of Peril
  Margin of Error
  Brink of Danger
  Line of Duty
  Legacy of Lies
  Secrets of Shame
  Refuge of Redemption

Cape Thomas Series:
  Dubiosity
  Disillusioned
  Distorted

Standalone Romantic Mystery:
  The Good Girl

Suspense:

Imperfect

The Wrecking

Sweet Christmas Novella:

Home to Chestnut Grove

Standalone Romantic-Suspense:

Keeping Guard

The Last Target

Race Against Time

Ricochet

Key Witness

Lifeline

High-Stakes Holiday Reunion

Desperate Measures

Hidden Agenda

Mountain Hideaway

Dark Harbor

Shadow of Suspicion

The Baby Assignment

The Cradle Conspiracy

Trained to Defend

Mountain Survival

Dangerous Mountain Rescue

Nonfiction:

Characters in the Kitchen

Changed: True Stories of Finding God through Christian Music (out of print)

The Novel in Me: The Beginner's Guide to Writing and Publishing a Novel (out of print)